P9-DCM-838

ANIMAL RESCUE TEAM
Show
Time

Read more Animal Rescue Team adventures!

Now available:

Animal Rescue Team #1: Gator on the Loose!

Animal Rescue Team #2: Special Delivery!

Animal Rescue Team #3: Hide and Seek

Also by Sue Stauffacher:

Donuthead

Donutheart

Harry Sue

ANIMAL RESCUE TEAM 4

Show Time

SUE STAUFFACHER

illustrated by
PRISCILLA LAMONT

A YEARLING BOOK

Sale of this book without a front cover may be unauthorized. If the book is coverless, it may have been reported to the publisher as "unsold or destroyed" and neither the author nor the publisher may have received payment for it.

This is a work of fiction. Names, characters, places, and incidents either are the product of the author's imagination or are used fictitiously. Any resemblance to actual persons, living or dead, events, or locales is entirely coincidental.

Text copyright © 2011 by Sue Stauffacher
Cover art and interior illustrations copyright © 2011 by Priscilla Lamont

All rights reserved. Published in the United States by Yearling, an imprint of Random House Children's Books, a division of Random House, Inc., New York. Originally published in hardcover in the United States by Alfred A. Knopf, an imprint of Random House Children's Books, New York, in 2011.

Yearling and the jumping horse design are registered trademarks of Random House, Inc.

Visit us on the Web! www.randomhouse.com/kids

Educators and librarians, for a variety of teaching tools, visit us at www.randomhouse.com/teachers

The Library of Congress has cataloged the hardcover edition of this work as follows:
Stauffacher, Sue.
Show time / Sue Stauffacher ; illustrated by Priscilla Lamont. — 1st ed.
p. cm. — (Animal rescue team)
Summary: Keisha's family's animal rescue center is asked to help at a nearby college that is being overrun with squirrels, while Keisha is trying to deal with her nervousness as she prepares for the regional jump-rope competition.
ISBN 978-0-375-85850-5 (trade) — ISBN 978-0-375-95850-2 (lib. bdg.) — ISBN 978-0-375-89794-8 (ebook)
[1. Squirrels—Fiction. 2. Wildlife rescue—Fiction. 3. Rope skipping—Fiction.
4. Family life—Fiction. 5. Racially mixed people—Fiction.] I. Lamont, Priscilla, ill.
II. Title.
PZ7.S8055Sh 2011
[Fic]—dc22
2010004759

ISBN 978-0-375-85134-6 (pbk.)

Printed in the United States of America

10 9 8 7 6 5 4 3 2 1

First Yearling Edition 2011

Random House Children's Books supports the First Amendment and celebrates the right to read.

For my nephew PFC John Carter Bateman,
who is serving his country in the U.S. Marine Corps

Chapter 1

Keisha Carter was crawling across the kitchen floor, trying to catch her little brother Paulo, when a cold swirl of outside air blew up under her sweater.

"Look at the snow in the glow of the streetlights, everybody." Daddy pulled Mama to him and gave her a quick kiss. "It looks like a snow globe."

"*Brrrrr* . . ." Keisha caught Paulo's ankle and gave him a kiss, too.

Mama rubbed Daddy's back. "Our truck is out in all that snow. I'll get the broom."

"Snow," Keisha told Paulo, pointing out the door.

"Rocket," he replied, pointing in the opposite direction as their puppy skittered down the steps.

"Daddy, you should close the door before—"

But Keisha was too late.

Paulo threw himself flat on the linoleum just in time to avoid a collision as Rocket bounded over the youngest Carter, then sailed through the doorway and out into the snowy white world.

"Hookey-hookey!" Paulo cried with a little scream of delight as he scrambled over to the doorway on his hands and knees to get a better look.

1

"Yep. He's doing the hoochie-coochie." Keisha caught the back of Paulo's sweater before he could launch himself out the door.

Rocket was on his back, shimmying in the new-fallen snow.

"That dog." Mama *tsk-tsk*ed, but she couldn't keep from smiling. Rocket was a cross between a coyote and a dog. The Carters owned him because he didn't fit in the wild OR the world of humans. He stalked prey and howled like a coyote, but he also loved humans like a domestic dog. Ever since the first big storm in December, he had demonstrated his wild side by rolling, burrowing and playing in the snow.

"All the girls in France do the hoochie-coochie dance, and the way they shake, it's enough to kill a snake." Keisha's six-year-old brother, Razi, step-tapped down the last two stairs and across the kitchen floor.

"Razi Carter," Mama scolded. "Did you hear that kind of talk on the playground?"

"No. Grandma taught me."

The puppy's head popped up out of a snowdrift, and Keisha could see that his perky ears and the ruff of fur that circled his face were now frosted with snow.

"I wish Grandma was here with her camera," Keisha said.

"Grandma is catching up on her beauty sleep." Daddy glanced at the clock. "But I need to go." He pulled on his coat and gathered his supplies.

The volunteers at Blandford Nature Center had asked Daddy to teach a class on repairing turtle shells at their annual Back-to-Nature Conference. He set off down the back steps, his arms filled with plaster shells, drills and screws.

Mama took the broom out of the closet. "I'll get Rocket and help Daddy with the truck. Razi, can you carry out the muffins? Without dancing?"

Mama couldn't send Daddy off to his first teaching job without food for the students. Growing up in Nigeria, Mama's family shared food as a way to show courtesy and to make friends. Daddy said it was one of the things he liked most about Mama—her friendly food.

"Can I wear the oven mitts?" Razi asked.

"You have to. The tins are still warm."

"Can I wear them to school?"

"We'll see." Mama and Razi put on their coats. She

was just about to follow her son out the back door when the office phone rang.

"I'll be there in a minute," Mama instructed Keisha. "Go ahead and answer it. Razi, I want you right back at the kitchen table after your delivery."

"C'mon, Paulo." Keisha took Paulo's hand and pulled him along into the office. She picked up the phone. "Carters' Urban Rescue," she said in her grown-up voice.

"No, no! The copier in the main office. The documents are there. Uh, sorry about that," a man's voice said into the receiver. "Can I speak to Fred? I'm an old friend. Bill Fox."

"I'm sorry, Mr. Fox. He just left." Keisha tugged on Paulo's hand. He was trying to get the stapler again.

"When will he be back? Sometime today?"

"Not until late, he said."

"That won't work. Darn it. The president wants someone on this today."

"Can I help? I'm his daughter. Is this about an animal?"

"Ummm . . . ani*mals*. Yes. About fifty of them. Maybe 150. Why they are my responsibility, I couldn't tell you. I'm the Director of *Human* Resources, not Animal Resources. You'd think this would fall under Groundskeeping or Physical Plant or Pest Control.

Melissa!" he shouted, causing Keisha to almost drop the phone. "Do we have a Pest Control Department?"

Keisha pulled out an intake form. "I'm sorry, Mr. Fox. I'm not sure I understand. What kind of animals?"

"Squirrels are taking over the campus here at Mt. Mercy College. They're frightening the students and making the nuns jumpy and, besides that, they're messy. Ms. Pontell, the president's secretary, just stormed into my office to inform me that his new Persian rug has teeny-tiny black walnut stains all over it . . . in the shape of paw prints! And *I'm* supposed to take care of it."

"The rug?"

"No, the squirrels."

It didn't help that Paulo had given up on the stapler and was now after the calculator. Keisha pushed all the office equipment out of Paulo's reach.

"So I thought, *I'll call Fred. He'll know what to do.*"

The back door slammed, and Keisha could see Mama holding a glistening Rocket and swatting the snow off her skirt.

"My mom will know what to do, too," she told Mr. Fox. "I'll go get her."

"What do you mean it needs more toner? I just put in a new cartridge. That's impossible. . . ."

Since Mr. Fox was already busy, it seemed like a good time to put the phone down. "Mama," Keisha said when she'd reached the kitchen. "There's a man on the phone who says he's Daddy's friend and the president wants him to take care of the fifty squirrels—or maybe 150—that are causing trouble over at Mt. Mercy and causing black walnut stains to get on the Persian rug."

Mama held out a dripping puppy to Keisha. "Fifty squirrels on a Persian rug?"

Keisha shrugged. It didn't make sense to her, either.

Rocket could wiggle his bottom and moan even when Mama was holding him in the air. Keisha grabbed an old towel from the basket by the back door and held out her arms.

"Oops. I left Paulo in the office. He was heading for the printer."

"All right, Ada," Mama said, using the nickname that meant "eldest daughter" in Mama's native language, Igbo. "Clean up this dog, eat your muffins with Razi and check his hands when he's done."

Keisha finished rubbing Rocket dry as Mama hurried down the hall to speak to Mr. Fox. Then she sat down in her chair, broke off a piece of banana nut muffin for herself and looked over at Razi, who, in about thirty seconds, had managed to become crumb-covered. Razi licked his fingers and pressed them to the crumbs on his plate, all the time tapping his feet on the floor.

"Razi, your tapping is shaking the table."

"I have to learn my steps. We're going to practice on the stage today."

"Can't you just think about them?"

"No." Razi continued to tap.

Keisha decided to focus on the warm, banana-y muffin in her mouth and not her brother. She was on her second muffin when Mama returned to the kitchen, put Paulo in his high chair and sat down next to him.

"That man needs to focus on one thing at a time," she said, tying on Paulo's bib.

"Can you help him, Mama?"

"I'm sure we can, but it's not an emergency. Your father is busy all day, and I promised Razi's teacher I would help her work on the costumes for the mid-winter show. We don't cancel our plans when it's not an emergency. We schedule an appointment."

"What about Grandma? We could go after she picks me up from jump rope practice."

"Grandma. Hmmmm . . ." Mama bit into a piece of muffin that Paulo held out for her. Paulo loved to feed Mama. It made him feel like a big boy. "Good idea, Ada. I will call him back and tell him that you and Grandma will come over this afternoon."

Keisha stared at her plate. Mentioning jump rope practice had made her lose her appetite. It was a big year for the Grand River Steppers jump rope team. Coach Rose called Keisha and her best friends, Aaliyah and Wen, the backbone of the team, as the oldest and most experienced jumpers. This year, they had a chance to win first place in their school district, which meant they would go to the district regionals in Detroit! And the team would stay overnight in the Renaissance Center hotel. The Steppers team went six years ago and they stayed on the sixty-fifth floor. They could see Canada!

Keisha and her friends had never stayed in the Renaissance Center hotel before. Marcus, Jorge, Zeke and Zack had all tried out for the team just in case they won a chance to go. Marcus and Jorge made the team because they'd both been in boxing club over the summer, so they were already good speed jumpers. Zeke and Zack Sanders didn't make the team. They were twins, and Grandma said one got both left feet and the other got both right feet. But Mama said not to repeat that.

Everyone agreed single freestyle was the hardest event, but Keisha loved it because you got to do dancing *and* gymnastics while you jumped rope. In freestyle, jumpers worked hard to make tricks look easy. Good freestylers could flow between one trick and the next, making as few mistakes as possible. Keisha loved the creative part of designing freestyle routines and picking out the dance music. It was *so* much better than boring speed jumping, which she usually placed in, too (though Aaliyah always beat her).

Last year at their school district tournament, she'd been the top placer in single freestyle. That was why Coach Rose had high hopes for Keisha in fifth grade.

But the more people talked about how good she was,

the more uncomfortable she felt. The point was Keisha didn't *want* to be the backbone! She wanted to be the pinky finger.

She watched Razi happily tip-tapping in his chair, licking his fingers like a cat.

Oh, to be in first grade again and not care whether you messed up or not.

In their last meet, against Cesar Chavez Elementary, Keisha had messed up twice during speed jumping and twice during her freestyle routine. Even though she jumped alone, her score counted toward the team's total points. Coach Rose had patted her on the back and told her it was okay, everybody had a bad day. But Keisha knew she'd let the team down. The problem was, she jumped fine in practice. She knew her routine in her sleep, but in front of all those people . . .

"Razi, do you ever get scared when you are up on stage?"

Razi stopped licking. "No! I like it. Wanna see my kabibble?" He jumped down from his chair and stood in front of Keisha, his shoulders back and his chin high. "Ms. Allen and Ms. Perry say you have to smile the whole time." Razi put on a big smile. He started moving his feet . . . slowly at first, then faster and faster. His feet were all over the place, but the top of his body stayed still. Keisha watched her little brother, her chin resting on her fist. She wondered how a kabibble would look in a freestyle routine.

"Want to see a 'kabibble'?" Keisha asked her friends Wen and Aaliyah that afternoon at the end of practice.

"Kabibble?" Wen pushed herself up. They'd been lying on the mats like a bunch of rag dolls, breathing hard because they'd just practiced their speed jumping.

"It looks something like this." Keisha stood and tried to imitate the step-tap combination Razi was doing that morning. "I was thinking . . ." She grabbed a jump rope. Instead of swinging it the way she did to jump, she kept the two ends in one hand and slapped the rope on the floor as she tried to imitate Razi's dance step. This was how the girls invented new moves for freestyle jumping.

Aaliyah stood up, too. She held out her hand to Wen and pulled her to her feet. The girls watched Keisha for a moment, trying to memorize the step. Keisha could get in a step and a tap between every *fwap* of the jump rope.

As the girls experimented, Coach Rose walked through the gym, talking to each team member about what they needed to focus on for their upcoming meet against C. A. Frost Elementary.

"Wen, have you been using that new wrist action we talked about?" Coach Rose made twirling motions with his fists.

"Trying." Everyone knew how hard it was to change the way you jumped. Coach Rose was working with Wen to better her speed-jumping times. "I start out doing it the way you showed me, but once I get going, I forget."

"Practice it in your head. You'll make the transition. Your feet are faster than your hands, and it should be the other way around. Oh, and, Keisha . . ."

Keisha twisted the ends of her jump rope, waiting. "Have you tried that synchronized breathing technique I taught you?"

Keisha nodded her head "yes," but she didn't look at Coach Rose.

"There's nothing to be ashamed of." He tilted Keisha's chin up so that they were looking at each other. "Everyone messes up, Keisha. Synchronizing your breath to your steps will help you focus on the job at hand . . . not on being nervous."

Keisha swallowed hard. *If only people didn't talk about it so much!*

"Don't worry, Key." Wen patted Keisha's back after Coach Rose left them. "You never had trouble before this year. You'll get your groove back."

Chapter 2

Even Grandma had to bring it up. After practice, she and Keisha took the number 17 bus over to the Mt. Mercy campus. Mt. Mercy was the biggest piece of "not city" in the city—even bigger than Riverside Park—so the Carters often got calls about wild animals from people who lived next to the campus. The grounds were filled with beautiful old trees of all kinds—black walnuts, elms, sugar maples. The Carter family had picnics there at least once every spring and fall, when the leaves looked their prettiest.

"So did you get those problems with your routine all fixed up?"

"Grandma, there's no problem with my routine. The only problem was that I messed up."

"I don't know if I would go so far as tha—"

Keisha stared out the window. "I got tangled twice during speed jumping and twice during my freestyle routine. I could do that routine in my sleep in fourth grade!"

"Keisha. Sweetie . . . take a cleansing breath." Grandma inhaled deeply, pressing her back into the bus seat and exhaling noisily through her nose. A lady with a shopping bag full of groceries on her lap turned to stare.

"Grandma, people are looking."

"Well then, let them learn something about the importance of the breath. Deep cleansing breath in . . ." Grandma blew out again . . . just as noisily. "Five . . . six . . . seven . . . releasing the tension . . . letting go of all the nervous energy . . ."

Keisha gave a big smile to the lady with the groceries before taking her own cleansing breath. Fortunately, they had reached the bus stop at the entrance to the college. Keisha pulled the wire to let the driver know they wanted to get off. "We're here, Grandma. Mama said to go to the administration building."

After they got off, Keisha tucked her chin into her jacket and studied the campus map mounted at the entrance.

Grandma scooped up handfuls of snow and tossed them over her head. "Look, Keisha! We're in a blizzard!"

Even though Keisha got chilled easily, the fluffy flakes were hard to resist: She plowed through a big drift of snow with Grandma right behind her.

"Would you like a snow cupcake?" Grandma asked, holding out a handful of snow.

"No, I think I would like a snow cone, please."

Grandma dropped the snow and grabbed another handful. "We're fresh out of snow cones, but today's special is a something-rather-new stew simmered slowly in my snow-cooker."

"That would be fine."

They *shush*ed along through the drifts until they came to the sign for the administration offices. Keisha and Grandma looked up at the tall brick building.

"It's like a gingerbread house with snow frosting," Grandma said.

Grandma and Keisha brushed each other off and

stomped the snow off their boots. Just as they were getting clean enough to go in, a big pile of snow fell out of the sky onto their heads.

"Vera Wang dang-doodle," Grandma said, peering up at the roof. "You're crushing my updo!"

"Uh, sorry about that. I usually shout 'Man overboard!' so folks know to get out of the way."

Keisha looked up to see a man in a knit hat with a pair of bushy eyebrows peering over the edge of the roof.

"Roof needs to stay clear so we don't get an ice jam up here," he called down to them. "But I have strict orders not to douse the pedestrians. Do you need assistance? I can come down . . . take you to the cafeteria and buy you a cup of coffee."

"Just look before you sweep next time!" Grandma called back. "You might douse an old lady!"

"Like I said, sorry about that."

Grandma and Keisha swatted the snow off each other for the second time before entering the old building. No one was sitting at the reception desk.

Grandma knocked on the molding. "I wonder if anybody's home," she said. "It's only four-thirty. I can't imagine they've closed up yet."

As if in answer to her question, an older woman in a business suit appeared in one of the doorways, a large purse dangling from her arm. She looked in their direction but did not seem to see them. Then she began digging in her purse.

"Excuse me. We're here to see Mr. Fox," Grandma said. "Could you point the way?"

"Oh dear. I can do better than that. I'll show you. I'm going just that way. It seems I've misplaced my wallet again, and I may have left it in the copy room. I'm Sister Mary-Lee. How do you do?"

Keisha shook Sister Mary-Lee's hand. If Sister was a nun, why wasn't she wearing a . . . ?

"The nuns here are Dominicans, dear. We don't wear the habit at Mt. Mercy." Sister Mary-Lee had a nice smile. "If that answers your question."

Keisha wondered if Sister Mary-Lee could read her mind.

"Are you interested in employment opportunities with us?" she asked Grandma as they proceeded down the hall.

"Not exactly," Grandma said as Sister Mary-Lee pushed the button for the elevator. "We're here to fire some squirrels."

"Those poor squirrels. I don't know how they're going to make it through the winter with the new rules in place."

"What new rules?" Keisha asked.

"Why, the memo came from the president himself. Students, faculty and staff were ordered to stop feeding the squirrels." She leaned down and whispered in Keisha's ear. "We were *asked* to stop feeding them last summer when Campus Safety began getting complaints that squirrels were harassing the students for food." Sister Mary-Lee straightened up. "The president will not tolerate emboldened squirrels."

The elevator stopped and Sister Mary-Lee stepped out first. "This way, ladies. Mr. Fox's office is next to the copy room."

As they walked down the narrow hall, a man rushed out of an open office door. "Melissa, I need those rejection letters! My phone won't stop ringing. This is what happens when you get four hundred applicants for a part-time posi— Oh . . ."

The man saw Grandma, Keisha and Sister Mary-Lee. He tugged on the waistband of his pants and tucked in the tail of his shirt. He was tall, with a shiny bald head covered in freckles. "Hello . . . sorry about that. Busy day."

"They're here to help with the squirrels," Sister Mary-Lee said. "You haven't happened to see my—"

"It's in my top desk drawer," said a young lady in a flowy skirt and ballet slippers who appeared in another doorway. She handed a stack of papers to Mr. Fox. "I found it by the coffeemaker," she said, smiling at Keisha and Grandma. "I'm Melissa."

"The coffeemaker?" Sister Mary-Lee looked once again into her purse, as if it held the answer to the mystery of her missing wallet. "I thought I left it by the copier. Hmmm . . ."

"It was open. My guess is you were contributing to the coffee fund. But all's well that ends well," Melissa said. She turned to Mr. Fox. "Good luck with the squirrels." Melissa touched her fingers to her mouth to cover her smile. "I'm sure your five o'clock appointment will be here shortly."

"Very funny," Mr. Fox replied to Melissa's back as she disappeared into her office. "Ladies, please come in."

Keisha had to press by Grandma to sit in one of the two chairs across from Mr. Fox's desk. He had a corner office. It was small, but it felt big because it had two windows that looked out over the trees and a courtyard garden. In the late-afternoon sun, Keisha could see the shapes of the statues covered in sparkly snow.

"Thank you for coming, ladies. Here's the 411." Mr. Fox sat down at his desk and adjusted the seat height. First he sank low, then he popped up so that his legs were stuck under the desk. "Darn thing," he said, more to himself than to Grandma and Keisha. "So . . ." He folded his hands and looked at them both, frowning.

"We have a lot of trees around here. And trees make nuts. And nuts bring squirrels. And to top it off, well-meaning people like our friend Sister Mary-Lee feed the birds and the squirrels and the chipmunks, too. So, what has happened over the years—"

But Mr. Fox didn't need to tell them what had happened over the years because, right on cue, a squirrel hopped onto the window ledge behind him and flicked

his bristly tail. And before they could say "kabibble," the squirrel had leapt up and caught the edge of the windowpane just above his head.

"What has happened over the years—" Mr. Fox repeated.

Even though he wasn't facing the window, Keisha could tell Mr. Fox knew what was going on behind him.

"As I was saying, our great founder, Mr. Charles Lowe, believed in the preservation of nature. . . ."

It was hard to pay attention to the history of the situation at the same time that a squirrel hung there, trying to catch his footing, his little feet banging up against the window.

"Heavens to Betsey Johnson." Grandma stood up and walked around the desk. She rapped on the window with her knuckle, but the squirrel just chattered at her. "He's a stubborn little guy."

"Please don't, Mrs. Carter. I've tried that already. I've shot rubber bands at the window and shined my telescoping shop light right in their eyes." Mr. Fox massaged the skin at his temples. "All I've managed to do is make one squirrel lose his footing and fall."

"Have you tried this?" Grandma unhooked the latch on the window and started to push on the sash.

"It's painted shut. Please come away from the window. I don't want to hurt him. I just want him to go away." Mr.

Fox turned back to Keisha. "Can you imagine what it's like to interview job candidates with a squirrel dangling from the windowsill behind your head?"

"Is *he* your five o'clock appointment?" Keisha asked.

"Yes! Around lunchtime and five p.m. almost every day, a squirrel shows up and tries to climb to the terrace above me. Sometimes it's more than one! It's very unnerving. I have no idea what he's trying to get to . . . there's nothing on the fourth floor but empty offices."

"Maybe . . . maybe someone is feeding the squirrels from a window above yours . . . ," Keisha suggested. "And that person goes there when there's no one else around."

"No, no. I'm sure not." Mr. Fox smoothed his hand over his head and adjusted his tie. "The woman who used to have this position put peanuts on the ledge out there. I think they're still hoping I'll do the same. But I can assure you that hasn't happened since I became human resources director. What do you think?" Mr. Fox asked. "Is there a safe way to discourage these squirrels?"

The squirrel was still outside doing pull-ups on the windowpane. Keisha wondered how long it could hang on.

"Keisha?" Grandma asked.

Keisha looked at Grandma. *She* usually talked first. "Um . . . I think the problem bears further study,"

Keisha said, which was the line that Daddy used when he wanted more time to think things through.

Finally, the squirrel managed to get his hind legs up on the windowpane. Now he was hanging upside down, looking in at them.

"Well . . ." Grandma cleared her throat. She sat up straight in her chair. "Squirrels have small brains, but maybe ninety-eight percent of that brainpower is used to fulfill one task, and—"

A loud scraping noise at the window interrupted Grandma. The squirrel had used the windowpane to launch himself into the cold winter afternoon. Grandma and Keisha stood up together, straining to get a look. They were relieved to see a squirrel, all in one piece, chattering at them from the branch of a nearby tree. He scurried up the trunk until he was out of sight.

Grandma leaned on Mr. Fox's desk and looked into his eyes.

"We have the bigger brains, Mr. Fox. The task before us is to outfox these squirrels. No pun intended, of course."

Chapter 3

Keisha helped Paulo up on the stool in front of the kitchen sink. Standing behind him so he didn't wobble off, she held his hands under the running water.

"Scub-scub-scub," Paulo sang as he slapped his pudgy hands together. Clean hands were always important, but they were especially important at mealtimes in the Carter family.

"Did you put the calabaza squash in the stew?" Keisha called out over her shoulder to Mama.

"Of course I did." The Carters' postman, Mr. Sanders, often brought Keisha exotic vegetables and fruits he found at the markets on his route. He'd started the habit when Keisha needed help with her geography. Something you could touch was much easier to remember than a list of cities and countries. Calabaza was a sweet squash from the Caribbean. If you started in Grand River, Michigan, and walked all the way down the United States, taking a left in the middle of the Gulf of Mexico, you'd probably meet a calabaza squash along the way.

"Calabaza-calabaza-watch-me-do-the-steptaraza." Razi heel-toed his way through the kitchen, letting the new word roll across his tongue.

"Hey!" Daddy lifted the platter containing the fufu—mashed sweet potato rolled into balls and fried—so it didn't meet Razi's bobbing head. "No tap dancing while we're getting ready for dinner."

"But it's more fun that way," Grandma said. She step-tapped to the table with the spoons and forks. Grandma liked to eat with her fingers like the rest of the Carters, but she also liked to keep her options open. "Where are the party parasols for the drinks? Do I need to make another trip to the Dollar Store?"

"I needed them to practice my cheers." Razi pulled two bedraggled parasols from his front pants pocket. "I want to cheer for Keisha next time she jumps rope so she doesn't get scared."

"I was *not* scared, Razi. I was nervous."

"Oh no." He tried to open one of the parasols but the tissue paper had torn. "This one's broken."

"Careful, everyone. This is hot." Mama put the steaming chicken stew in the middle of the table. Daddy set his platter next to hers. The smell of cinnamon and sweet potatoes filled the room and drew all the Carters to the table.

As Mama put the stew into bowls and Keisha helped Paulo into his seat, Grandma announced: "I will say grace." She sat down and folded her hands. Before everyone had a chance to sit and spread a napkin on their laps, she said: "Dear Lord, thank you for the bounty of this food, for the farmers who grew it and the wonderful cooks who make it smell so good. And, if you don't mind, can you transfer a little bit of the nerve we saw in that squirrel today to our Keisha? Amen."

"Hmmmm . . ." Daddy poked his thumb into a ball of fufu and spooned a bit of chicken and rice into it for Paulo. "I was going to tell you about my turtle-shell class, but before I do, I think I better hear about this squirrel."

"Can I have the floor first, Daddy?" Having the floor meant Keisha got to talk all by herself—no interrupting.

"Of course you can."

"I would like to ask everyone to please *stop* talking about my nerves. It's making me more nervous." As she made her little speech, Rocket jumped up and put his front paws on Keisha's lap. She patted Rocket's head. What was it about a puppy that made you feel good even when you felt bad?

Right then and there, Keisha made a decision. "Rocket's the only one who can give me advice."

"That's not fair," Razi said.

"Nair." Paulo banged on his tray.

"Good idea, Key," Daddy said. "Watch Rocket tonight and see if he isn't the most in-the-moment member of this family."

"He's not in the moment. He's in the kitchen." Razi dropped his mound of sweet potato into his bowl of stew and pressed it below the surface. "With us."

"Maybe you need a squirrel on the Grand River Steppers. Think of the tricks he could do, especially if he was hungry." Grandma proceeded to tell the Carters who were not in attendance about the squirrel outside Mr. Fox's office window.

"Ee curl," Paulo said, popping a piece of his fufu in his mouth.

"You can see the squirrel tomorrow." Grandma reached over to wipe the dribble off Paulo's chin. "I'll put you in the papoose and we'll do some investigating on that campus. Our new friend, Sister Mary-Lee, told us the squirrels are scaring the college students."

"Paulo can go tomorrow, but *I* can't," Razi said. "I have tap-dance practice after school. *I'm* going to be one of the boys doing the Bojangles stair dance."

"You mean *the* Bill 'Bojangles' Robinson stair dance?" Daddy asked.

Mama leaned over and picked up the napkin Razi had dropped to the floor when he made his announcement. "I thought you said the third graders were doing the stair dance."

"My music teachers, Ms. Allen and Ms. Perry, say I'm advanced." As if to prove it, Razi tapped his toes against the side of his chair. "My costume has a tail."

"Back to the squirrels for a minute, bucko . . ." Daddy speared another ball of fufu with his fork and dropped it on Paulo's tray. "This happened last summer. Don't you remember, Fay? Mom, it was when you took the kids to zoo camp. Fay and I went out and talked to the head of the Grand River Veterans Affairs Facility. What was his name, Fay?"

"Lieutenant Washington," Mama said. " 'Squirrels gone wild,' I think he called it."

"Right. The guys in the rehab program were feeding peanuts to the squirrels, and they got too tame."

"How did they solve their problem?" Keisha asked.

"They stopped feeding them. It takes a while, but it usually works."

"But Sister Mary-Lee said they stopped feeding them last summer. Right, Grandma?"

"They were *asked*. That is different from they *stopped*. Something's amiss at Mt. Mercy," Grandma said. "No self-respecting squirrel puts on a show like that without food as a goal. I tell you it was worthy of a circus."

One of the good things about snow was that you couldn't get too serious about jump rope at lunch. Everyone had to wear their boots and the blacktop was wet. That meant Keisha and her friends could goof around—play freeze tag, do handclaps or jump double Dutch just for fun. But you had to keep moving because it was cold! Though she loved to play in the snow, Keisha's hands were always the first to turn to ice inside her mittens.

"Come on," she said to her friends Wen, Aaliyah and Jorge. "We gotta do something to warm up. Let's handclap."

Wen stood in the middle of her circle of friends. "Let's do it shoulder-to-shoulder so we get some body heat, too. We've still got five minutes."

They leaned against the side of the school in a line and did "The Long-Legged Sailor," patting their own knees, then patting the friend on the right, then the friend on the left.

Have you—ever, ever, ever—in your—
    long-legged life—
Seen a—long-legged sailor—and his—
    long-legged wife?

Keisha liked "The Long-Legged Sailor" because they tapped faster and faster as the rhyme went on, and you couldn't help but warm up with all the arm-pumping and getting your knees slapped. They'd finished "short-legged" and "pigeon-toed" and were on "bow-legged" when Ms. Tellerico came out with her arm around a tall, thin girl in a skirt. Her long, dark hair might have kept her shoulders warm, but Keisha could see goose bumps on her pale legs.

Everyone stopped clapping to watch them come across the playground. Nobody wore a skirt in the dead of winter—at least not without snow pants.

"Something tells me that girl is not from around here," Aaliyah declared.

"From the way she's dressed and the look on her face, she must come from someplace warm and sunny." Wen straightened up.

"Hello, FFGs." Ms. Tellerico used the nickname their teacher, Mr. Drockmore, gave his class. "FFGs" stood for "Fantastic Fifth Graders." "I want to introduce you to Savannah. She just moved here and she'll be in your class, but she needs a buddy."

"Looks like she needs a hot-water bottle." Aaliyah tugged on her puffy jacket.

Ms. Tellerico continued, "Keisha, I think it's your turn to be a Langston Hughes Ambassador. I thought you could give Savannah the tour after recess."

"Can we go in early since she's in a skirt?" Keisha asked, hopping up and down.

"There are only two minutes to the bell, and you know if I let you in, every second grader is going to beg me—"

"It's all right," Savannah told her. "I can take it."

Even with her chattering teeth, the children could hear Savannah's Southern accent.

"Where you from, Savannah?" Aaliyah asked after Ms. Tellerico rushed off to help someone who'd slipped on the ice.

"Alabama."

"Alabama? Me too! Well, my people are."

"I saw you handclappin'. Do you know this one?" Suddenly Savannah was a whirl of motion. She clapped her hands on her thighs, then crossed her arms and hit her shoulders before smacking her hands flat on her hips. She had leg motions, too. Heel-toe-rock, heel-toe-rock.

Hear my name—Savannah Jane—Ask me
    again, I'll tell you the same.
What do I eat?—Pig's feet—What do I drink?—
    Black ink.

Then, just as suddenly as she'd started, Savannah stopped. "Whew," she said. "That's better than standing around freezin'."

Aaliyah nodded, clacking her braids together. "We don't use our feet when we're handclapping. You had yours going in every different direction." She jumped up and put her hand on Savannah's shoulder. "Show us again."

Keisha and Wen looked at each other. It wasn't so easy to earn Aaliyah's respect.

"I can do better than that. I'll teach you so we don't freeze to death."

Even though it was fun to learn a new way to hand-clap, as soon as the bell rang, the FFGs rushed to line up.

Ms. Tellerico tapped Keisha's shoulder on the way into the building. "I'll tell Mr. Drockmore you two will be a little late. Why don't you show Savannah the library first?"

Keisha and Savannah followed the class upstairs to the 4–5 wing, where Keisha took off her boots and mittens and jacket. Then she took Savannah down the hall to the library. "This is my favorite place in school," Keisha told Savannah.

They went through the big double doors. The library was empty and quiet and warm as toast. Keisha curled up in one of the big armchairs by the picture windows. Savannah sat next to her, staring out at the street below. They could see the A.M.E. Church, the Baxter Community Center, even as far as Ron's Hand-Done Car Wash two blocks away.

"It takes a little getting used to. . . ." Savannah's voice trailed off. "All this city, I mean."

"What are you used to?" Keisha asked.

Savannah jumped up and ran over to Ms. Wilson's book display at the entrance to the library. She came back with a book about farms.

"This," she said, holding it out for Keisha.

It was just a little kid's book, filled with pictures of tractors and cows and chickens.

"You lived on a farm in Alabama? Why did you leave?"

"My mama and daddy . . . they got a divorce. And the farm has been in Daddy's family since the Civil War." Savannah looked at Keisha as if she expected her to say something. But Keisha didn't know what to say.

"Beau's in college already, and little Benny had to stay back to help with the chickens. Eggs . . . that's our main business. But Mama wanted a fresh start, so we moved up here to be with her people for a while."

Keisha studied the book. "It's so different," she said.

Savannah flipped the pages to a picture of a man riding a horse, herding cows into a pen. "That's what I miss most . . . my horse, Sugar." Savannah sucked in her lips until Keisha couldn't see them anymore. "Double rats," Savannah said when she'd opened her mouth again. "I swore I wouldn't cry on the first day."

"It's okay." Keisha patted Savannah's red knee. It was still cold from being outside. "I cried in the library once. Marcus dropped the *Webster's* dictionary on my toe."

"Did it swell up?"

Keisha nodded. "Big! I had to go to the school nurse and elevate it during math."

"You got to miss math . . . that was good timing."

"Yup," Keisha agreed, even though she liked math. "And it was better by art time. It had to be! We were painting ceramics."

The V.A. facility was across the street from Riverside Park. All summer, whenever the Carters went to Too-Tall's Cone Stand, they had to walk a different way to avoid the construction. That's because a park with a fountain, a gazebo and handicapped ramps was being installed on the side nearest the rehabilitation facility. Daddy said some local businessmen and women who had served their country raised the money for the park to be built. They wanted to make it a little nicer for those who had to recover from injuries. Next summer, when the weather was nice, the patients could go out in wheelchairs and sit by the fountain in a grove of trees. For the winter months, they'd installed a sunroom with a big picture window that overlooked a ravine and gave a good view of the new bird feeders.

"Look, Daddy." Keisha pointed. "They must have finished the construction this fall. Doesn't the gazebo look pretty all covered in snow? You can't even see the stream anymore."

"It does look nice." Daddy's eyes traveled from the

gazebo to the building. "I didn't realize the bird feeders would be so close to the picture window. I need to remind Harold to put up some decals so the birds don't fly into that big piece of glass."

Daddy looked down and ruffled Razi's hair. "Hey, big thinker. Don't suck on your mitten. That defeats the purpose."

"But I'm remembering my steps." Razi ran up the long walk to the entrance to the hospital. Heel-toe-shuffle-dip. Looking down, he jumped up as if climbing a stair, tapping his way up invisible steps.

"Hold up there, mister. Don't dance me off my feet." Keisha and Daddy had been watching Razi, so nobody saw the man coming around the corner. He wasn't using crutches, but what looked like two short sticks to help him walk. One of his legs seemed twice as big as a normal one and had a funny bulge at the knee.

"Sorry about that," Daddy apologized, jogging over to where Razi and the man had almost collided. "Razi, come over here. You need to watch where you're going, buddy."

"No problem," the man said. "I'm told I'll be able to do that someday, too. But for now, I'm more tippy than tappy. Sergeant Pinkham, at your service. But you can call me Sarge."

"Good to meet you, Sarge. Fred Carter. And these are my children Keisha and Razi."

"Is Razi our little Fred Astaire?"

Razi looked up at Sgt. Pinkham. "I'm not Fred Astaire. I'm Bill 'Bojangles' Robinson and I'm practicing my stair dance. Do you want to see?" Razi didn't wait for his audience to decide; he ran ahead to the real steps at the entrance to the hospital.

"If you don't mind, I'll sit down for this." Sgt. Pinkham brushed off one of the benches that flanked the walk and sat down. Keisha could see that it hurt him to move from the way he pressed his lips together when his bottom found the bench seat.

"It's not so much the walking but the uneven ground. I'm waiting for a better sleeve."

"I'm sorry." Daddy took a seat beside Sgt. Pinkham. He patted the space beside him, but since Keisha didn't have her snow pants on, she stood next to Daddy at the side of the bench and leaned on his shoulder.

"I'm not quite following you," Daddy said. "A sleeve to help your leg feel better?"

"That's the word they use for the fitting between my real leg and my artificial one. When I try to walk on the snow, this one rubs against my skin . . . it's like . . . well, like a shoe that doesn't fit right."

"How long since . . . ," Daddy started to ask, but then his voice trailed off.

"I got hit by an IED—that's an improvised explosive device—while delivering supplies outside of Kabul last March. Four pieces of shrapnel lodged in my lower leg. They've tried to save it. I've had twelve surgeries. But a couple of months ago, the docs decided my only two options were to fuse my ankle together or to take off the lower leg entirely. It was a hard decision to make, but I decided to have my leg removed. With all the new prosthetic technology, I'll be able to do a lot more with an artificial limb than a damaged real one. It's only been a month since that surgery, so the stump's a little tender."

"You had it removed. . . ." As he talked, Daddy pointed at Sgt. Pinkham's knee, which caused the man to flinch to avoid being touched.

"Funny thing," Sgt. Pinkham said. "Even when it's not there, I try to protect my injured foot from getting hurt."

"I've read that amputees can still feel the limb that's been removed."

"You mean the phantom toes?" Sarge reached out as if he was going to massage his foot, but rubbed his thigh instead. "I sure can. Sometimes I wake up at night because of the itching. Other times, I feel like the toes are all twisted together. It's really strange."

They stopped talking for a minute and watched Razi as he rocked back and forth, tapping the step with his toe, jumping up two steps, down one, then tapping across.

"Those little foot movements seem like such a miracle to me now," Sarge said after watching a minute. "I guess I took all that for granted until, well . . . until I couldn't anymore."

"Sounds like you've been here awhile," Daddy said. "Did you grow up in Grand River?"

Sgt. Pinkham laughed. "Nosireee Bob! I grew up in the mountains of Colorado. My mom and my sister fly out once a month to see how I'm coming along, but I miss them *almost* as much as I miss the mountains." Sgt. Pinkham winked at Keisha to show he was joking.

A rustling sound in front of them caused Keisha to jump in surprise. A fat, bushy squirrel holding an apple core was perched on the edge of a garbage can just across the sidewalk.

Keisha pressed into Daddy. The squirrel was so close she could see little huffs of warm breath coming out of its mouth.

"Familiar little guy," Daddy remarked. "In fact, that's why we're here."

"Larry is why you're here?"

Daddy glanced at Sgt. Pinkham. "Larry? Are you talking about the squirrel?"

"He may be any old squirrel to you, but to me, he's my friend Larry. Like I said, my family's far away, and I don't get out much. . . . Hey, buddy."

"But how can you tell who is who?" Keisha asked.

"Because they do look different if you pay attention. Larry's tail looks like it was dipped in brown paint."

Larry chirped at the humans watching him, almost as if to say, *Don't bother me now—I'm busy*. Then he proceeded to eat his apple. Keisha watched, amazed. Larry gnawed his way around the apple core,

turning the fruit with his finger-like paws and then
flipping it upside down to get at the bottom. All that
was left before he dropped it and scampered away was
the stringy piece in the middle. He'd even eaten the
seeds.

"Hmmm." Daddy rubbed his chin. "Very interesting."

"Uh-oh." Keisha pointed to the hospital entrance.
"Razi found someone else to almost run into, Daddy." A
man had rushed out of the building and nearly collided
with Razi. As Razi chattered away—not unlike the
squirrel—the man watched him with a puzzled expres-

sion. Keisha bet he was wondering what a little kid was doing tap-dancing on the hospital steps in the middle of winter.

"Stay here, Key." Daddy ran over to Razi and struck up a conversation with the man. They shook hands. From the way the man clapped Daddy on the shoulder, Keisha thought they must know each other.

"That's the director of the facility. Lieutenant Washington. Former Navy man. Good guy," Sarge told Keisha. "A little too much spit and polish for my taste, but a good guy." Sarge used his hands to re-position his leg. "Mmmm, that's better. My stump was falling asleep."

Keisha stole a glance at the place Sarge's leg must have been cut off. She could see the outline of the "sleeve" that he'd been describing earlier.

"Want me to explain it?" Sarge asked her, patting the bench to invite Keisha to sit beside him. "My experience is that kids have a lot of questions about amputations, but they don't think it's polite to ask."

Keisha nodded. Sarge was right. She never would have asked on her own, but she was curious.

So Sarge told her how the shrapnel had damaged not just the bones but the tendons and, even more important, the arteries. "Arterial flow, they call it. It's how the blood circulates through your body, and the blood is what delivers the oxygen. My arteries were so damaged that it was like my foot had trouble breathing." Sarge burst into a hearty laugh. "That sounds strange, even to me. But maybe you have a question I haven't thought of. . . ."

He was right, of course. Keisha had about ten questions, but she wouldn't dare—

"Ask one."

"What do you miss being able to do most?"

"That's easy. Climbing. I did a lot of rock climbing before I joined up." Sarge smiled at the memory. "What would you miss the most?"

"Jump rope." The answer came automatically to Keisha, but then she wondered if that was true anymore. "Maybe," she whispered.

"Why maybe?" Sarge scooted closer to Keisha. "If you don't mind my asking."

Later, she told Wen she couldn't believe she was telling a perfect stranger about her biggest problem. But he had such a kind look on his face while she explained her jump rope worries that it was easy.

After Keisha finished, Sarge said, "That is a big problem. I'd like to think on that one, if I may."

"Okay," Keisha agreed, but it didn't seem like a very big problem compared to Sarge's.

They sat in silence, watching Lt. Washington show

Razi how to do a military salute. After Lt. Washington and Daddy shook hands again, Razi tore down the steps and over to Keisha and Sarge.

"Lt. Washington wants me and my dance class to perform for the troops!" Razi was so excited he almost slipped on the pavement clicking his heels together to salute Sarge.

"Maybe if I have my new sleeve, you can teach me a step or two."

"Maybe." Razi didn't seem sure. "But I don't know how to dance with a pirate leg."

Chapter 4

As soon as they got to the Baxter Community Center that evening for their 4-H Wild 4-Ever meeting, Razi yanked his hand out of Keisha's and ran to find Big Bob. Big Bob was the leader of the Grand River 4-H Club, devoted to learning about the wild animals that lived in the city. He was also Grandma's boyfriend, but she hadn't decided yet if he was "the one."

Keisha searched the room for Savannah and found her standing alone near the dessert table. Though she

usually sat on the big comfy couch with her friends and Grandma, Keisha went over to join Savannah. Big Bob had called that afternoon to ask if Keisha would introduce their newest member to the group.

Razi was the first to draw attention to the big box of wood scraps sitting on the front table. "Is that new business, Big Bob?" he asked, pointing.

"Why, yes it is," Big Bob responded.

"We're going to use it to build birdhouses," Zack Sanders informed Razi as he bounced on the big couch.

"I call the hammer!" Zeke started bouncing, too.

Razi was between them on the couch. Pretty soon, they looked like the row of mechanical ducks that popped up and down at the shooting gallery of the Green County Fair. Mama said the Sanders twins were good at getting Razi going.

"*And* it's not our only new business," Big Bob reminded the boys. "We need to welcome a new member all the way from Alabama—Savannah Dernier—plus, we need to discuss a perplexing squirrel dilemma at the Mt. Mercy campus."

"And we need to eat my Grandma Alice's dessert!" Razi called out without raising his hand at all.

"I call the meeting to order, please." Big Bob smacked a hammer on a block of wood. "Old business comes first. Aaliyah needs to report on the public-information campaign we just wrapped up. Aaliyah?"

Big Bob scootched his seat over to the whiteboard.

Aaliyah stood up and tugged down her hoodie. She went to the front of the group. "On November twenty-second, we had tables outside the Nantucket Bakery, Kingma's Market and Family Video," she said. "We also put flyers on people's doors. In case you weren't there, Jorge is passing around the flyers now."

Keisha glanced down at her flyer. Marcus had drawn a picture of the young deer with the plastic pumpkin that got stuck on its head at Halloween time. He had also drawn a few other pictures from sources he got on the Internet. They included a raccoon with its head trapped in a peanut butter jar, a cat with its head stuck in a hubcap and a baby skunk with its head wedged in a soft-drink cup. Keisha had thought up the title of the flyer: "Is your trash a trap? Think about it!" Underneath, the Wild 4-Ever kids had listed three ways to avoid these problems. 1) Keep the lid on your trash. 2) Keep your recycling indoors until recycling day. And 3) Keep an eye out for potential wildlife hazards in your neighborhood—like six-pack rings, jars and disposable cups—and throw them away!

"So, in conclusion," Aaliyah continued, "our public-information campaign was a capital B-I-G success. We educated seventy-two citizens face-to-face and put doorknob flyers on 136 houses. Marcus and I are creating an info sheet for 'Trash Trackers' to put on the 4-H Web site. If you want to hear what we've written so far—"

"Wow, that's impressive." Big Bob jumped up and clapped. So did the rest of the Wild 4-Evers. Zeke whistled. Razi hooted. Zack pounded the armrest of the couch.

Aaliyah seemed surprised that her report was already at an end, but she was a good sport about it. "I will entertain your further questions during cinnamon twist time," she said, and walked tall back to her seat. Obviously, Aaliyah had peeked under the aluminum foil on Grandma's dish.

"Excellent work, Aaliyah. As the folks at Carters' Urban Rescue tell us, education is the key to preventing many wildlife mishaps. Well, I think that's it for old business. The first item of new business would be . . ." Big Bob squinted at his palm, where he'd written the agenda. "Ah, yes. The squirrel shenanigans over at Mt. Mercy College. I was *hoping* . . . um . . . that club member Keisha Carter would give us a report."

Mmmmm. From across the room, Grandma got an eye scolding from Keisha. She had told her granddaughter that *she* would fill in the Wild 4-Evers. Grandma just shrugged.

Savannah gave her a gentle push on the shoulder. "That's you," she whispered.

Keisha hadn't been nervous during "old business" because she didn't know she'd have to give a report. As much as Aaliyah liked all the attention on her, whenever Keisha had to make a report, she had the same fluttery feeling she got before she performed her freestyle program. She took a big breath.

"Alice thought you'd like to make the report, sweetie." Big Bob looked sorry. Grandma was avoiding Keisha's eyes.

"Some people need more practice performing," Grandma whispered loudly to the boys surrounding her.

"Keisha has good nerves," Razi told Zack and Zeke. "She practices them a lot."

Keisha felt her knees go weak. The breath still hadn't come out.

All of a sudden Keisha felt Savannah standing next to her. She was pressing her shoulder into Keisha's. Keisha *knew* how she was going to introduce Savannah because she'd practiced what she'd say with Mama. "Savannah is from Montgomery Springs, Alabama, and her favorite 4-H activity was working with horses. She did dressage."

Keisha and Mama had never heard the word "dressage" before, so they looked it up on the Internet. It was a special kind of horseback riding, and it was pronounced *druh-SAHZH*.

Savannah took Keisha's hand and looked into her eyes as if asking her: *Do you need help?*

Did Southern girls understand eye language?

Her mouth was completely dry, though she did manage to breathe out and back in again. She gave Savannah an eyes-wide look that meant—*Yes . . . help!*

"Can I say something about squirrels at the University of Alabama?" Savannah asked Big Bob. Savannah's Southern accent took all the attention off Keisha. Some of the kids giggled.

"Sure," Big Bob answered, looking just as relieved as Keisha that she was off the hook.

"My big brother, Beau, goes to the U of A. Once, during Family Week, we were sitting on the lawn of the quad having a picnic, and a squirrel hopped up on the table and drank out of my cousin's juice box."

All the kids laughed about this.

"Did he use the straw?" Marcus asked.

"Well, how else do you drink out of a juice box?"

Keisha wasn't sure if it was the image of a bushy squirrel slurping juice or the way everyone was cracking up that got her tongue unstuck from the bottom of her mouth.

"At Mt. Mercy, they're running at the students and begging for food. They're trying to get into the college administration building. They dangle on the window ledges and leap from the trees onto the side of the building. Mr. Fox, the man we talked to, said it's hard to do business."

"He could pull down the shades," Zeke suggested. "That's what we do when the Pipers use their leaf blower and get dirt on the side of our house."

"My dad threw his shoe at a squirrel that was sitting on our grill," Marcus added. "The bad part was his shoe went over the fence and the Thomases weren't awake. When he tried to climb their fence, their dog Trixie tore his pants."

Even Wen had a squirrel story. "I watch the squirrels drop black walnuts on the driveway. I think they mean to bury them, but a lot get left on the driveway and then there's a big mess."

While the kids were talking, Big Bob was taking pieces of wood out of the box and playing with how they fit together. Keisha wondered where they came from. They were all different sizes and shapes: angled ones that looked like a set of stairs, long thin ones and blocky pieces.

Big Bob let the group hear from all the Wild 4-Evers who wanted to tell their squirrel stories. After they were done, he said: "I understand that Mr. Drockmore has been teaching you about if-then hypotheses in science lab. I'm wondering if we could make some hypotheses about what is happening at Mt. Mercy."

"*If* you feed squirrels," Zack said, jumping up to sit on the back of the couch, "*then* they come back."

"Yeah." Zeke jumped on the back of the couch, too, to show his agreement.

"How about: *If* you are outside and you have

food, *then* you'll see squirrels," Aaliyah suggested.

Grandma raised her hand. "May I add something?"

Big Bob held his hand up for quiet. "Alice Carter has the floor."

Grandma made her way to the front of the room. She squared her shoulders.

Keisha and Wen had an eye giggle. "It's Grandma Professor time," Wen whispered.

Grandma cleared her throat. She was waiting for Perfect Hear-a-Pin-Drop Quiet. The Wild 4-Evers became a little less wild. All this had to be over before they could get to cinnamon twist time.

"In my long association with the squirrel community, I have found that squirrels enjoy a narrow band of activities. They include chattering, chasing, burrowing, burying, gnawing, nibbling and, last but not least, napping. The most frequent of these is gnawing and nibbling on nuts, seeds, berries and, yes, grill grease, or to put it more accurately—our trash."

Grandma rubbed her hands together. She was just getting started, and Keisha knew that when it came to animals, she had a lot to say. Zeke and Zack slid down the couch back until their heads rested on the cushions. It might be boring, but they knew not to interrupt Grandma when she was on a roll.

Unless you were Keisha. Aaliyah reached forward

and tapped her on the shoulder. "I'll give you a box of Lemonheads if you save us from a Grandma Professor lecture," she whispered.

Keisha loved Lemonheads. Whenever they went to Charley's candy store, she picked up a box of Lemonheads and sometimes Pixy Stix and sometimes SweeTarts. But *always* Lemonheads. She raised her hand. "Can I talk again, Grandma?"

"If you come up here with me," Grandma said.

Keisha shuffled up to the front of the room. Grandma pushed her forward a little but kept her hands on Keisha's shoulders. "Um, they probably will never get rid of all the squirrels because they have so many trees at Mt. Mercy. The biggest problem is squirrels acting crazy around the administration building. But they're not going to cut down the trees, so . . ." Keisha glanced out at all the kids. Looking at them looking at her made her decide to keep studying the floor for a while. "My if-then would be . . . *If* there are lots of trees around the building *and* that means a lot of squirrels, *then* you just have to make sure they can't get into the building and find a way to live in peace."

"I vote for peace!" Big Bob said.

"Since there are trees all over campus," Keisha continued, thinking out loud, "I wonder why the administration building is the only one they complain about at

Mt. Mercy. According to what Daddy says, '*If* squirrels are crawling all over a building, *then* there is food involved.'"

"Yes!" Grandma squeezed Keisha's shoulders. "To test this hypothesis, we must conduct a thorough search around the administration building for squirrel-friendly food. Like in Dumpsters and such."

"Like cinnamon twists!" Razi shouted. "We better eat them before the squirrels find them."

Chapter 5

The next day after jump rope practice, Keisha and Savannah stood just inside the school doors watching for their rides. Savannah had asked Keisha if she could watch jump rope practice. They didn't have a team in Montgomery Springs.

Outside, Marcus and Jorge were climbing the huge snow pile the plow had made on the side of the blacktop.

"Coach is always easy on us the day before a meet," Keisha explained. "That's why we just did five-minute speed-jumping rounds, worked on the group jump and practiced our freestyle routines in slow motion."

"You did so well in practice," Savannah said. "So what happens at the meet?"

Keisha scuffed her boots against the rubber doormat. She got very interested in which boy would be "king of the hill."

"I was just asking because I used to get real nervous when I jumped . . . with Sugar . . . but I, well, I found some things that helped."

"But you were on a horse!" Keisha said. "He was the one jumping, not you." During the two days Keisha had spent as Savannah's buddy, she had learned something about 4-H dressage. Dressage was a test of how well your horse could perform certain tasks, like stopping, turning and jumping, in response to your commands.

"The competition is how well you do as horse *and* rider. I found that if I was nervous, so was Sugar. I would stiffen up, and then I connected differently to him . . . do you see what I mean?"

Keisha shook her head. "Did it really matter if you were a little stiff as long as you stayed in the saddle?"

Savannah tapped her finger against her lips. Then she grabbed her backpack and stuck it between her knees. "Watch." She bent down a little and rocked her shoulders back and forth. "You have to use your imagination, but watch my legs. When everything's loose, I can hinge up here—that's a riding word. It means . . . um . . . flow. My body can respond to the horse and the horse to my body. When I'm tight"—Savannah tightened her legs—"look what happens up here."

The girls heard a pop, and Savannah let her backpack fall to the floor.

"Uh-oh! I think I just busted my lunch box." Unzipping her backpack, Savannah stuck her hand inside and fished around. "When you get nervous, you tighten. If I tighten on Sugar, then he gets nervous, too. Like last night. When you were surprised you had to stand up and talk, I pressed up against you all relaxed. Didn't that help?"

Keisha thought back. She remembered Savannah's shoulder. It did help.

"Ew." Savannah held up a squished sandwich. "I hate egg salad, but I promised Mom I'd bring home anything I didn't eat."

Keisha crinkled her nose. It didn't smell too good, either, having been in her backpack all day.

"She probably won't want it now." Savannah tossed the smushed sandwich in the trash can.

"I know your rope isn't a live thing like Sugar. But as I watched you practice your freestyle routine, I noticed that when your coach was looking, you messed up. And when you started again, you got stiff, and that changed the way you turned your rope. . . . Oh my gosh, there's my mom." Savannah waved at a little red car parked in the bus lane. "Hope she hasn't been waitin' long."

Marcus took advantage of Savannah's opening the door to get back in without having to buzz the office. "Colder than it looks," he said, stomping his boots on the rubber mat. "What's that stinky smell? Smells like rotten eggs."

"Savannah was trying to show me how getting nervous messed up her horse routine, and she smushed her sandwich."

Marcus gave her one of his "girls are crazy" looks, where he pulled his head back like a turtle and flared his nostrils, so Keisha tried to explain how the smell of rotten eggs was connected to Savannah's getting stiff in dressage.

"Hey, I think I know what she's talking about," Marcus said when Keisha had finished. "When I fade back to shoot, if I try too hard, I mess up. But when I just let it flow . . ." Marcus went through the motions of shooting the basketball. "Score!"

"Flow! That's the same word Savannah used. So, how am I supposed to stop thinking about being nervous? Especially when everybody is always bringing it up?"

"Easy." Marcus tugged the bottom of Keisha's ear. "Just turn off your brain. That's the off switch right there."

"Ha, ha. There's my grandma. Gotta go."

Keisha gave Marcus a backward wave as she ran down the front walk before hopping into the truck.

"I'm starving, Grandma. Did you make something sweet for after dinner?"

"I did. I made pumpkin spice cake."

"Can I have a little when we get home?"

"We're not going home yet," Grandma said. "We've got to make an emergency stop."

"Really? Please don't. I'm *so* hungry."

"Heavens to Betsey Johnson, Keisha Carter. I knew you would be." Grandma handed Keisha a square of pumpkin spice cake wrapped in wax paper. The smell of nutmeg and cloves erased the yucky memory of warm egg salad sandwich.

"This will tide you over while we swing by the college. A squirrel broke into the president's office today and caused pandemonium at Holmdene Hall."

"How?" Keisha tried to picture a fat, bushy-tailed squirrel scurrying through the big double doors and into the president's office.

"Dropped right from the ceiling, swung on the chandelier and knocked over the president's family portrait. At least that's the way his secretary reported it. Ms. Pontell. She's one of those high-pitched-jump-on-a-chair screamers, and we all know they sometimes miss the most obvious clues. The little guy didn't hang around long." Grandma held tight to the wheel and concentrated on getting the big truck down a narrow street lined with cars. It had snowed four more inches the night before, and the roads were slippery.

"You should relax, Gram. You'll turn better," Keisha said through a mouthful of cake.

But Grandma wasn't listening. She loved a big to-do. "A real halls-of-higher-learning hullabaloo," she said happily.

"If the squirrel didn't stay around, where did it go, do you think?"

"Well, it didn't leave by the front door. Ms. Pontell said it disappeared into thin air. That's what they want us for. To figure out the point of entry and seal it up."

The truck tires crunched up the main drive to Mt. Mercy. As they were getting out, a woman rushed outside without a hat or coat on. She was as tall and straight as a pencil.

"Oh, thank heavens you're here. I wanted to clean all surfaces right away, but President Kellogg said I should leave them untouched. I'm Ms. Pontell."

Keisha and Grandma watched Ms. Pontell shiver and waited to hear more.

"So we didn't destroy the evidence, you see. Follow me, please."

She led the way into the president's office, a big room filled floor to ceiling with dark-paneled walls and tall bookcases. "It's a rodent, I told him. Plain and simple. Cuter, maybe, but a rodent nevertheless . . ." She stopped to draw in a big breath. "Putting its grimy little paws on the presidential family portrait! Who knows where those paws have been?"

At the far end of the room, Keisha almost missed the man sitting behind the massive desk. He turned in his chair and tilted his head to the side. "These are the squirrel catchers, I presume, Ms. Pontell?"

"Yes, President Kellogg. I'm so sorry to interrupt. What a day."

"That will be fine. Thank you, Ms. Pontell."

The president stood up. He was a short man, with a round face and round glasses and hair that traveled from one side of his head to the other. Tucked into his tweed coat, he looked a little like an owl to Keisha. Or maybe it was the way he stood there blinking at them.

"So this is where the breaking and entering oc-curred?" Grandma strode across the room with her hands clasped behind her back.

Keisha and President Kellogg watched as Grandma examined the room, running her hand across a bookshelf, gazing up at the chandelier, then down at her feet, where the picture had crashed to the floor. Careful not to walk in the broken glass, Grandma picked up the frame and examined it.

"You have a lovely wife, President Kellogg. I'm Alice Carter of Carters' Urban Rescue. And this is my granddaughter, Keisha. She specializes in small rodents."

Why did Grandma say things like that?! Now President Kellogg was looking at her all funny.

"Thank you," he said. "Tell me, don't you wear special clothing to catch wild animals?"

"Oh, we do. We absolutely do. But we thought it would be best to first ascertain the point of entry and exit. It might help if you explained what happened."

"Well . . ." The president tugged on the lapels of his tweed coat, remembering. "Ms. Pontell was giving me some letters to sign. She noticed it first. 'Swinging from the chandelier,' I believe she said. Then I looked up to see it jump to the bookshelf . . . that's where it knocked over our portrait. When Ms. Pontell started screaming, it just seemed to disappear behind the books."

"Which books, exactly?"

"Why . . ." President Kellogg pulled off his glasses and polished them with a handkerchief. He gazed at the floor. "I believe it was in the Shakespeare section."

"I see. Well, we'll need a ladder to investigate further."

Keisha stared at Grandma. Not many people knew, but Grandma Alice was afraid of heights. She would ride at top speed down the sledding hill at Richmond Park or swim out to the sandbar at Millennium Park, but Grandma never climbed to the top of the slide and she never climbed trees, ladders or fences, either. It made her feel woozy.

"In the meantime, can you give us a description of the squirrel?"

President Kellogg picked up the phone and asked for someone named Penny in Physical Plant. "Please tell Jim to bring a stepladder to my office," he instructed.

"You must be joking, Mrs. Carter," he said when he'd hung up.

"Not at all. I'm quite serious. How long was it? What color was it? How bushy was its tail?"

"I don't see what difference it makes . . . isn't a squirrel a squirrel?"

Keisha thought asking Grandma that question was like asking a college president, *Isn't a book a book?*

"President Kellogg, there are several species of squirrels in Michigan: The red and eastern gray squirrels can be found on both Michigan peninsulas, whereas the southern flying and eastern fox reside only on the Lower Peninsula. Lastly, the northern flying squirrel can be found on the northern Lower Peninsula and entire Upper Peninsula. These squirrel species have a variety of habitats and are important parts of our natural heritage. However, I will limit my remarks to the squirrels I have seen on your campus: the gray, the fox and the red. . . ."

Keisha was trying to hide a yawn as Jim came in with the ladder. As soon as she saw him, Keisha guessed he was the same man who'd dropped snow on them the other day, but she couldn't be sure because this time he wasn't all bundled up with earflaps on.

"This is our handyman, Jim Kleinschmidt," President Kellogg said as Jim set up the ladder.

"Oh dear, I don't have my bifocals on. Keisha," Grandma instructed, "please climb this ladder and tell me what you see."

"I can climb it for you," Jim offered.

"No thank you." Grandma put a hand on his shoulder. "Keisha is trained in what to look for."

Keisha wondered what training Grandma was talking about. All she knew was that a squirrel could squeeze through a hole the size of a quarter. . . . Well, Daddy said a little one could.

She went up the ladder looking for quarter holes.

"Does our insurance policy cover children?" Keisha heard President Kellogg ask Jim.

"I'm happy to do it," Jim answered. "Squirrels don't bother me. In fact, I like the little fellers."

"Don't under-estimate Keisha," Grandma said, loudly enough for people in the hall to hear. "She is a trained professional."

"At her age?"

"I'm ten." Keisha ran her finger along the bookcase. Did they ever dust up here? She sneezed. Mama wouldn't like it at all. Even with all the animals and people in and out, Mama made sure the Carters kept their house as neat as a pin.

"Goodness gracious." Keisha looked down to see Sister Mary-Lee peering up at her. "What is Keisha doing on that ladder? Is it perfectly safe?"

"Nothing is perfectly safe, Sister Mary-Lee," Grandma said. "Even standing outside this building." The way Grandma looked over at Jim, Keisha thought her guess about who had dumped the snow on them was right.

"It was me who snowed them," Jim said, twisting his hat in his hands. "I said sorry."

"I don't understand." Sister Mary-Lee looked to the president for clarification, but he was trying to help Keisha find the right place.

"I think we'll need to move the ladder a little. Shakespeare would be in Drama, just over here, next to English Literature."

"Well . . . ," Sister Mary-Lee continued. "I will leave you to your work. I forgot to get the proofs for the *Alumni Magazine*. And you know how particular Mr. Fahey is about typos."

"I see. Jim, I notice that Keisha's fingers are covered in dust. I'll hold this ladder steady while you get some wood polish and a dusting cloth. Any progress up there, young lady?"

Jim left the room with his head down. *The poor guy keeps messing up*, Keisha thought.

"Not yet." Keisha went back to examining the shelf. Nothing had touched down on these shelves for a long time. A cold draft of air blew by her cheek. She looked up to see a ceiling vent with the metal cover hanging loose.

"Or maybe . . ." Keisha leaned over and tried to push the cover back into place. Crumbles of plaster fell onto the president's Persian rug.

"What's going on up there?" Grandma wanted to know. "Is that the cold-air register?"

"Oh my, oh dear . . ." Sister Mary-Lee was at a loss for words. "I'll get the dustpan."

Keisha started down the ladder. As she hopped off, Sister Mary-Lee returned, pan in hand. There was a flurry of activity as the president and Sister Mary-Lee worked to clean up the plaster.

"It would be much safer to examine that register from the floor above," Sister Mary-Lee said. "And that's where I need to go. I'll take you two ladies there on my way to get the proofs."

"Wait a minute, Sister." Grandma took the dustpan out of her hands and picked through the plaster. She held up a powdery peanut shell. "President Kellogg, I doubt you eat peanuts and throw the shells on the floor."

"I can't have that near me. . . ." President Kellogg backed away. "I most certainly do not. I am mildly allergic to peanuts. I never eat them."

"Well, squirrels do. And if you have a peanut allergy, it's even more important that we get to the bottom of this"—Grandma pointed up—"by going to the top of this. . . ."

"Oh, Mrs. Carter," said Sister Mary-Lee. "I'm not sure a woman your age—"

"Not the ladder. The building, as you suggested.

We're right behind you." Grandma emptied the pan into the president's waste can.

"I'll take this as well," she said, and carried the trash can along with her. "We may find more clues. Keisha? Coming?"

Keisha followed the older ladies out the door.

"I can't imagine . . . ," Sister Mary-Lee fussed as they got into the elevator. Grandma pushed the button. Keisha noticed she pressed #4, not #2, but she didn't say anything. Grandma must have a plan. "There haven't been peanuts in the building since . . . We all know not to bake anything with peanuts."

Grandma and Keisha glanced at one another as the elevator went up. These peanuts were their biggest clue so far.

"And even with the whole ones, we never went anywhere near the president's office. Oh dear," she said as the elevator doors opened. "This is the fourth floor."

"Well, as long as we're here . . ." Grandma stepped out of the elevator. "I know you're busy, Sister Mary-Lee, but we need to have a look. I'm sure President Kellogg would approve. Keisha?"

"Me too." Keisha took Grandma's lead. "If peanuts make the president sick, then we really have to keep them out of this building."

"Well, I wouldn't say sick, but they do make him

flush. He gets red from his chin to the top of his head. But how will being on the fourth floor help?"

"Take us to the room that would be above the president's office."

"But the president's office is on the first floor. We're on the fourth."

"Is this the top floor?"

"Why, yes it is."

"And can we get out onto the flat part of that roof?" Grandma asked, peering out the window in the hall.

Once again, Keisha wondered what Grandma was up to . . . the thought of going out on the roof must give Grandma the willies.

"Oh, I don't know about that. I've gone out there, of course, but not since . . ." Sister Mary-Lee stopped herself. She looked as if she'd just been caught doing something wrong.

"What is it, Sister Mary-Lee?" Grandma handed Keisha the wastebasket and took the sister's hand. "What is it you're not telling us?"

"Well, on a nice summer day . . . or even sometimes in the winter, I used to climb out and toss peanuts down to the squirrels. We have bird feeders on the campus. Why not squirrel feeders? It doesn't make sense. The poor things. I believe they're all the same in God's eyes. And I'm not the only one."

While Grandma and Sister Mary-Lee were talking, Keisha fished around in the garbage can. Amidst the balls of crumpled paper, the plaster dust and a few broken pencils, she found a piece of tar paper. That was strange. And it looked like it had been nibbled! She jammed it in her pocket to discuss later with Grandma.

"But you stopped feeding them, didn't you?" Grandma prompted Sister Mary-Lee.

"Of course. It was a direct request from the president."

"And what did you do with the peanuts?"

"I don't remember. I must have asked Jim to bring the barrel down."

"Are you sure?"

"Well, yes, I think I'm sure, but when I get very busy . . . I don't know . . . things sometimes slip through the cracks. Maybe I didn't." She paused. "Oh dear. If it's up there now, it will be under a foot of snow."

Unless someone found it when they were clearing off the roof, Keisha thought, *someone who liked the little fellers a lot.*

Grandma undid the window latch and pushed up the window. "Keisha, dear, be a good girl and lean out this window. Tell me if you see any peanut barrels lying around."

Chapter 6

Keisha walked into the gym at Aberdeen Elementary and tapped the rubber mat three times for good luck. The stands were already full. There were seven schools in their district, and since she'd started jumping in third grade, the crowds at the district meet had grown bigger every year. Only one team would advance to the district regionals. Last year, it was Cesar Chavez. But this year, Langston Hughes had a good chance to win.

Keisha was competing in three events: single speed, double-Dutch speed and freestyle. She took a belly breath and looked up into the stands. Grandma Alice was in her cheerleading uniform, a snazzy tracksuit she'd found at Encore Consignment and sewed "Steppers #1" onto in the school colors. Mama and Daddy were next to her. Daddy held Paulo, sucking his fingers and looking wide-eyed at the crowd. He must have just awakened from his nap. Mama was scanning the stands for Razi. Her eyes met Keisha's and she waved to her daughter.

Where was Razi? Keisha shook her head. Not her problem. She went over to her teammates, huddled together in the corner, and pressed in between Marcus

and Jorge. Everyone put their arms around each other and leaned in so that Coach Rose—who was kneeling in the middle of the circle—could give his last instructions.

"Marcus, Aaliyah, Jorge, I'm hoping for a personal best in the speed jumping. Keisha, Wen, Lindsey, you all have the potential to place." Coach Rose went through every member of the team and gave them a goal to shoot for.

When he got to the freestyle jumping, Keisha noticed he didn't mention her name first, as he usually did. Instead, he said, "Marcus, even though it's new, your routine can place if you ace it."

Marcus stepped on the handles of his rope and smiled at the ground. "Keisha's the one who made it up."

"And you're the one who's going to nail it." Coach Rose put a hand on Wen's and Keisha's shoulders. "FFGGs"—the extra G was for the girls—"now is your time to show these other jumpers what fierce competitors you can be—here *and* in Detroit."

When their coach had finished, the Steppers dropped their ropes and piled their hands in the center on top of his head. "One—two—three." Coach Rose signaled the cheer.

"Steppers, step out! Gooooooo, Steppers." The Langston Hughes side of the bench erupted in cheers. Grandma gave Keisha a Grandpa Wally Pops whistle, high and shrill; it always got her looks.

Aaliyah threw her arm around Keisha as both girls put their hands over their hearts for the playing of the national anthem. The music made Keisha think of Sarge and the other vets at the facility. Maybe, if they scored top points today, she'd ask Daddy if Sarge could ride along to the district regional meet in Detroit.

As the music died down, people took their seats, but Grandma remained standing, making her hands into the shape of a megaphone. "Cat walk, dog run, get out there and have some fun!"

This brought a big cheer from the crowd. The meet had officially started. The girls went over to the far corner of the gym where the speed-jump heats would be happening. Aaliyah and Wen would compete here first. Keisha had her freestyle event first, but she could warm up for that anywhere.

Aaliyah started jogging up and down, bringing her knees up to her navel. Wen used her rope, alternating slow and fast rotations.

The jumpers from Aberdeen were fast. So were the kids from the Southeast Academic Center. They seemed to have gotten even faster since the individual meets. Aaliyah didn't appear to notice the other jumpers at all. She'd grabbed a rope and was doing easy double unders.

"Want to warm up on double Dutch for speed?" Aaliyah asked. Keisha could see that her friend's forehead was already shining. She grabbed a towel out of the bin.

"I want to do a few moves from my routine first." Keisha patted Aaliyah's forehead. Her hair was braided with her lucky competition beads. "At least the advanced ones," Keisha said. Coach Rose wouldn't let them put a move into their routine until they could hit it nine times out of ten. Keisha faced the wall and went through the harder parts of her program: side-step crisscross into a scissors crisscross, sideways bell, knee-to-shoulder, drop-down squat jump—

"Keisha Carter, Renee Proha, Emmarene Johnson." Keisha listened to the names being called out over the loudspeaker, an indication that it was time to report to your event. She felt something heavy squeeze in between her tummy and her throat. As she trotted over to the freestyle event, Keisha tried to remember to breathe.

She sat cross-legged at the edge of the mat, waiting for the judges to finish scoring a jumper from C. A. Frost. When they looked up and motioned to her, Keisha stood up, tapped the rubber mat with her foot three times for luck and jogged to the middle of the taped-out square.

Just as she was about to say "Judges ready?" she caught a glimpse of her brother swinging from the side of the bleachers. He dropped to the floor, ran around, scrambled up three stairs and launched himself into Daddy's arms.

"Go, Key! Go, Key!" he screamed, waving his tiny parasols in crazy circles.

Keisha focused her eyes on the floor, trying to block out the distraction. "Judges ready?" she asked the table.

"Judges ready," came the answer.

She looked over at Coach Rose. He started her music. Keisha took a deep breath and swung the rope. Grandma whistled.

After that, it was all a blur. Later, she remembered doing the basic jumps she'd included to get warmed up: tiptoe skip into a twister for four beats, then a half turn, then a crisscross. But somewhere near the beginning, a thought crept in. She'd kept the cancan turn into a heel skip in her routine. It was coming up. Just the thought made her swing her rope faster. Before she knew it, the rope caught her toe. Keisha started again. She moved into her cancan turn. Her legs felt like lead! After three kicks, her rope caught her toe again. Keisha wanted to run off the mat, but the music kept going. She had to finish.

"Go, Key! Go, Key!" she heard Razi yell just before she finished. She tried to lift her head up and smile at the end, but all she could manage was a nod before scrunching up her shoulders and running off the mat.

Out of the corner of her eye, she saw a couple of the Aberdeen Skippers watching her. They didn't make fun of her bad performance. You could see they felt sorry for her.

That was almost worse! If only Razi hadn't distracted her!

The rest of the meet rushed along. Keisha did all

right in single speed jumping, but she got tangled in the rope twice during double-Dutch speed. That had *never* happened before. The way Aaliyah yelled encouragement had never bothered her before, either. In fact, hearing her friend's encouragement every few swings had always kept Keisha's energy high: "Hit it! You got it! Harder, Key!"

But today, the way Aaliyah yelled put her off her rhythm.

"Next time, don't shout out," she told Aaliyah as they walked off the floor.

"What? That's my job. All the twirlers shout out."

"Well, don't."

"Girl, if you're looking for someone to blame for messin' up, point that finger back at yourself."

Razi was the first Carter to reach her. He threw his arms around Keisha.

"You got tangled up in your nerves again, Key. Here's a hug."

Keisha shrugged him off. "If you weren't fooling in the bleachers, I might have done better. Mama, Razi acting crazy messed me up! Don't let him come next time."

"What about me?" Grandma asked. "I was yelling louder than Razi. Should I not come, too?"

Daddy handed Paulo to Mama. "Fay, can you get a

ride with Mr. Sanders and the boys? I promised the folks over at the V.A. facility that I'd put up some decals to protect the birds from their picture window. They've already had one collision. I'll take Keisha with me."

Despite her poor performance, Marcus, Jorge and Aaliyah had all scored personal bests, giving Langston Hughes just a few more points than Cesar Chavez and winning them a spot in the district regional meet in Detroit.

High fives, chest bumps, back claps were traded back and forth. But not with Keisha. She was so mad she didn't even say good-bye to her friends. Once she was in the truck, she realized she was still holding on to the jump rope she'd used in the speed jump.

"Daddy." Keisha smacked the rope against the glove compartment. "You can't let Razi come to the district regionals. He made me mess up."

Daddy didn't answer for a moment. He fiddled with the heater and rolled down the window, using his gloved hand to wipe the ice crystals off the side mirror.

"Something for you to think about, Key," he said, backing out of their space in the school parking lot. "Razi ran all over the gym last year, just like the other kids his age. It's a long time to sit still. But most important, honey . . ." He paused and, without taking his eyes off the road, put his hand on Keisha's arm.

She shrugged it away.

"It's never bothered you before. Are you sure Razi is what's making you—"

"I don't know what it is! Everything is making me jumpy—"

Daddy laughed. "That's a good thing. It *is* a jump rope competition, after—"

"Not in a good way." Keisha wished Daddy wouldn't laugh . . . *or* give high fives to Marcus and Jorge, who both placed in speed jumping even though it was their first year on the team.

They entered the drive to the V.A. facility. As they drove toward the main entrance, Daddy spotted Sarge all bundled up, sitting on a bench in the sun.

"Why don't you visit with Sarge while I install these decals? It will be good for you to get some sunshine and fresh air."

"Fine." Keisha jumped out of the truck without another word.

"Well, hello, Miss Carter. How nice to see you. How is the squirrel situation going over at the Mt. Mercy campus?"

"Okay." Keisha didn't bother to brush away the snow. She hopped onto the bench and studied her mittens. "Well, not okay, really. One got into the president's office with a peanut, and he's allergic."

"Still . . ." Sarge gave a long, cat-like stretch and closed his eyes. "You should never take your job too seriously. Or it can affect your not-job. At the moment, it's a beautiful February day. The sun is shining, the snow is sparkling. But you look like you have a storm cloud over your head."

Sarge re-arranged himself on the bench to try to find a more comfortable position. "Unless this has nothing to do with squirrels at all. I see you have your jump rope with you."

Keisha looked over at Sarge. His kind eyes were all it took to make her pour out the misery of the day. "It's the safest routine I've done all year! Coach just wanted me to jump clean. But I couldn't even do that."

"I'm sorry, Keisha. I know how important it was for you to do well for your team."

A fat teardrop balanced on Keisha's eyelid. She had wanted so much to be the backbone Coach Rose had asked her to be.

"Does this mean you don't get to go to Detroit?"

"No. We still won because Marcus and Jorge got first and second in speed jumping. We just beat Cesar Chavez."

"That's great!" Sarge held up his hand and Keisha got a high five after all. "When do you go?"

"The district regionals are two weeks from Tuesday."

"So you have another chance. That's excellent news! I have some good news, too. I got my new sleeve."

"Really?" Keisha brushed her cheeks with the backs of her mittens.

"Yup. This baby brings new meaning to the phrase 'perfect fit.'" Sarge tugged on his pant leg to show Keisha. "Wanna hear how they made it?"

Keisha nodded. She scooted closer to Sarge and examined the shiny plastic cup that fit snugly to the end of his leg, just below his knee.

"A doctor took a wand filled with sensors and rubbed it all over my stump. Like this . . ." Sarge demonstrated by rubbing his left hand all over his right fist. "I watched on the computer screen as the wand communicated information about the contours of my stump and built a three-dimensional model in the exact same shape. Every little mole or fold of skin was included. So now there's no rubbing at all. Pretty soon, my new walking foot will arrive and I can start learning to walk again. I mean, I do know how to walk, but I'm going to learn with my custom-made foot."

Keisha sat back. Sarge was like a little kid, so excited to be learning how to walk again. She crossed her arms and tilted her chin to feel the sun on her face.

"But what's even better is that since this sleeve fits my leg perfectly, I can attach all kinds of artificial feet to the other end and each one will feel comfortable right away. They have special feet for different uses. When I've saved up enough money, I can buy one that will let me climb again."

"You can climb up mountains again?"

"Sure I can. Climbing mountains is the same as

walking from here to the entrance of the building, Keisha. One step at a time. Hey, look. It's Larry."

Keisha followed the direction of Sarge's finger to the moving puffs of snow that Larry kicked off the branches as he leapt from limb to limb.

"I don't know what it is about these guys . . . but they lift me up, you know? They're carefree. And they don't mind doing the same darn thing over and over and over. They're always straining and struggling to climb the bird feeders—did I tell you that Lt. Washington had to install raccoon guards because the squirrels here are so tenacious that the regular squirrel guards didn't work? I think about how stubborn they are when I'm trying to bend and stretch in physio.

"Problem is, I can't really see them from inside. That's why I come out here whenever it's not too cold. We haven't had too many days like this one." Keisha and Sarge watched Larry find an acorn still clinging to the tree. He smoothed his tail along his back like a big, fluffy scarf. After he'd finished nibbling the acorn, he pressed his body flat along the limb, as if he was going to take a nap.

"You know what, Keisha? I just thought of something. When I was a climber, I competed a lot. I wanted to be the best. After a while, I found that it meant so much to win that I started getting nervous before a competition. So nervous that sometimes I threw up. That would sap my energy and make it harder to scale the verticals.

"Somewhere along the line, I realized I'd gotten off track. I mean, I didn't start climbing as a young kid to earn trophies. I decided that at the next event I would just enjoy myself—basically that I would let myself lose if that's what having fun cost me. Having fun became my goal—not winning. So I relaxed and just got into it."

"Did you go with the flow?" Keisha asked, remembering her conversations with Savannah and Marcus the day before.

"Yes, exactly!"

"What happened?"

"I didn't win. Not even close. But I had more fun at that meet than I'd had in the whole past year. I liked climbing again. The same as when I was a kid. And after a while, I started winning, too."

Sarge re-adjusted his pant leg so that it fell back down around his false leg. "Now, going back, my challenges will be different. I know I can't do things the same way. I'm going to have to learn to think differently . . . be a little better about taking my time. But I can still have fun. Like our friend Larry up there."

"Keisha!" Daddy had stepped out the door of the

V.A. facility and was waving his arms at his daughter. "Want to come in here and check my decal placement?"

Keisha was ready. She couldn't even feel her rear end, it was so numb from sitting on the snow.

She hopped down and gave Sarge a big hug. "Next summer, I'll bring my friends Aaliyah and Wen and we'll teach you how to double-Dutch," she promised before skipping up the sidewalk to join her dad.

"What did you and Sarge talk about?" Daddy asked as he led her down the corridor and past the nurses' station to a big sunroom with floor-to-ceiling windows on three sides.

"The flow," Keisha said, smiling at Daddy's puzzled expression.

Whatever the flow was—and Keisha wasn't sure she could describe it yet in words—it was happening outside the windows of the new sunroom at the V.A. facility. Men and women sat in their wheelchairs beside low coffee tables, observing the birds flitting from bush to tree to feeder. Goldfinches clung to the thistle netting, and nuthatches climbed the suet feeders. Bright red cardinals swooped in for a quick bite at the sunflower-seed platform.

Keisha searched the woods for squirrels. Sarge was right. The ones on the ground were too far away to admire their bright eyes and bushy tails and silly squirrel antics. If only there were a way to bring them close without their messing with the bird feeders so that Sarge and the other vets could enjoy them year-round.

"What do you think?" Daddy put his arm around his daughter.

"I love it. It's like a wildlife show."

"All birds, all the time. But I meant, what do you think about my decals?"

"I think you need a few more down low. Remember the cardinal that ran into our courtyard window at school? That was right near the bottom."

"Good point." Daddy peeled another decal from its backing.

"Then I think maybe we should go home so I can say I'm sorry to Razi."

Chapter 7

"Marcus, when did we switch from social studies to architecture?" Mr. Drockmore was walking around checking student work. They'd been assigned a "mind-mapping" exercise to find a good topic for their reports on the Civil War. He picked up Marcus's paper and studied it closely. Then he held it out for the class to see. "Please enlighten us about this structure . . . and how it connects to your Civil War report."

Marcus twisted his pencil eraser inside his ear and crinkled his nose. He always did this when he got embarrassed. "I got my mind map done on the other side. I was just doodling to keep from disturbing others."

"Oh, well, then. Congratulations on the speedy completion of your assignment." Mr. Drockmore flipped the piece of paper over. "Back to work, everyone."

Once again, heads went down and pencils were picked up. Keisha liked doing mind maps. You wrote down three things you wanted to learn more about, and then you asked questions about each thing. Then you asked questions about the questions, narrowing your subject down until you got a good idea for your paper.

Mr. Drockmore kneeled next to Keisha. "Do you

mind asking Marcus some clarifying questions?" He placed the mind map Marcus had done on Keisha's desk. "In the meantime, I'll let Marcus look at yours. . . ."

"Sure, Mr. Drockmore." Keisha's writing and Marcus's drawings often got tacked up on the PMA board ("PMA" stood for "positive models of accomplishment"). When students were really good at something, Mr. Drockmore often asked them to help other kids "step up their game." Keisha looked at other people's writing, and Marcus critiqued posters before they were displayed.

Keisha studied what Marcus had written. "Guns. Carrier Pigeons. Tents." Under "Guns," he'd written, "What kind?" Under "Pigeons," "How come they didn't just fly away?" Keisha brainstormed more questions for Marcus to ask. After she'd come up with a few, she flipped over the page to see what Marcus had drawn.

It was a house built with crazy-sized pieces of lumber. Hey! She recognized those pieces. They were from Big Bob's box of odds and ends. The box had been donated by their friends who worked in the woodshop at Downtown Senior Neighbors' Community Center. At the last meeting, the Wild 4-Evers had decided the pieces weren't big or standard enough to make birdhouses, so they planned to save them for a big s'mores roast.

But it looked as if Marcus had other ideas. Could birds live in these? Keisha let her mind wander. This was the sort of house Razi would enjoy living in. He could climb from one perch to the other. In her mind, Keisha saw him leaping through the bleachers. He frolicked like a . . . like Larry the squirrel!

Mr. Drockmore rang the bell on his desk, which signaled that it was time to get ready for lunch.

Keisha rushed over to Marcus. "Will you bring this to lunch?" she asked, slapping the paper on his desk, house side up.

"You want to talk about the Civil War while we're eating? It's pizza day."

"No. I want to talk about a squirrel circus."

Marcus stood up and grabbed the back of Jorge's shirt as he passed by. "Have you ever noticed how hard it is to follow a girl's brain in motion?"

"Mr. Fox. When we write up our report, we're going to title it 'The Case of the Missing Peanut Barrel.'" Grandma sat back in her chair across from Mr. Fox's desk and crossed her arms, a satisfied look on her face.

"Is that so?" Mr. Fox was eating a peanut butter and jelly sandwich—and talking—without offering Keisha or Grandma anything to eat. It was four-thirty and Keisha's tummy was grumbling. Again.

He must have heard the growly noises. "Sorry. I never got to eat lunch today."

"Yes, well . . . there's a peanut theme running through this whole case. And where there are peanuts . . . there are certain to be squirrels. Keisha?"

Keisha pulled a clear plastic bag out of her backpack.

"A bag full of snow?" Mr. Fox asked.

"It wasn't easy, I can assure you . . . but here's the evidence." Grandma took the bag and picked through the snow to find a soggy peanut shell. "These are all around the base of the administration building, Mr. Fox."

Mr. Fox removed his glasses and examined the shell up close. "So you think students are eating these around the building? And attracting the squirrels?"

"No. I do not. Keisha, show Mr. Fox what you found the other day."

Keisha pulled the piece of tar paper out of her pocket and handed it to Mr. Fox.

"This looks like roofing paper," Mr. Fox said, "that's been torn off the roof."

"Keisha found it when we swept up the debris in the president's office."

"I don't know why it would be in his office," Keisha said. "Unless an animal brought it in through the duct-work. And I don't think it was torn, either. Look close. Those are nibble marks."

Mr. Fox set down his sandwich and wiped the corners of his mouth with his thumb. "You don't mean to suggest that squirrels are nibbling our roof? This can't taste good!"

"A young squirrel will try anything when it's hungry in wintertime," Grandma replied.

"Let's go back to the peanuts. If students aren't eating them . . . and we know no one is feeding them— president's orders . . ." Mr. Fox slapped his hands on the desk. "You're not suggesting that it's raining peanuts, are you?"

"Yes, I am." Not to be outdone by Mr. Fox, Grandma slapped her hands on her thighs. "In fact—"

"It rained some peanuts just now, Mr. Fox." Keisha pointed out the window over Mr. Fox's head.

"You're having me on, Miss Carter."

"We're not, Mr. Fox," said Grandma. "Your back is always to the window, but we think it's been raining peanuts on a regular basis around here. You don't have to believe us. Check the evidence yourself. There's a peanut on the ledge outside your window right now."

Mr. Fox twirled around and bounced out of his chair, just in time to meet a squirrel landing on the ledge and nabbing the peanut. "Well, I'll be a monkey's uncle," he declared as the squirrel chattered at him before leaping to the safety of an oak tree. Returning to his chair, Mr. Fox rubbed his bald head, thinking.

"It's raining peanuts. But why? And how?" He rubbed so hard he made the skin turn pink. Keisha watched Mr. Fox's expression go from confused to angry. "And who would do such a thing? Surely not Sister Mary-Lee?"

"No . . ." Grandma stroked her chin in a very wise way. "I don't believe so. Sister Mary-Lee stopped feeding the squirrels when the president asked her to."

Keisha's tummy grumbled in a very not-wise way.

She had a fleeting thought about leaping on Mr. Fox's desk, grabbing the uneaten half of his sandwich and rushing off with it like the squirrel.

"Sometimes when people are lonely, Mr. Fox, they try to make friends with animals," Keisha told him. "That's what happened at the veterans' hospital. It could be happening here, too."

As Mr. Fox turned to gaze out the window again, Grandma winked at Keisha. They both had a suspect in mind, but decided it was better for Mr. Fox to come to his own conclusions.

Razi Carter was about to make CFH, or Carter Family History. Daddy had sung in the musical *Oliver!* at the Civic Theater, Grandma had had a walk-on part in *MAMMA MIA!*, even Keisha had taken a turn as "excess waste" in their school play about the environment—though she had a garbage bag over her head at the time. This was the first time a member of the Carter family had a lead role in a public performance. As with all recipients of a CFH Award, Razi got to choose the sweet. He'd been thinking about it since Mama had "remembered it" to him.

"Let's go to Sweetland and buy M&M's in designer colors," he suggested as the Carter family finished an early dinner so that Razi wouldn't be too full during his dance routine. "No, wait." He shook his head. "That lady wasn't nice to me."

"You can't blame her for enforcing the rules. You stuck your hand in the bin." As soon as she'd cleared her place, Grandma had begun filing her nails. She planned to wear her green velvet coat and her favorite emerald ring, which Big Bob had given her. In honor of the emerald theme, she was painting her nails "ruby red," just like the color of Dorothy's shoes in the *Wizard of Oz* movie.

"Ummmm . . ." As Razi thought, he tried to touch his nose with his tongue. Paulo imitated his brother.

"Ummmm . . . ," Paulo said. He gave up and pressed his nose flat with the palm of his hand.

"I'm still the only one who can do it," Keisha informed her brothers, expertly sticking out her tongue and tapping the bottom of her nose with it. "If I were you, Razi, I'd pick The Cone Shop and get ice cream. Your cone won't melt at this time of year . . . even if you dawdle."

"I know!" Razi jumped out of his chair. "We'll go to Charley's Crab and have the inside-out German chocolate cake!"

"Excellent idea." Daddy took Paulo out of his booster seat and swung him in an arc around the room.

"No!" Razi held up his finger. "I want to go to Marie Catrib's and have the carrot cake. That's my final final."

"You don't have to decide your final final until after the show," Mama reminded Razi. "You just can't change your mind after we start driving."

Since Rocket got excited whenever Daddy swung Paulo or when Razi hopped up and down, the Carters' puppy was now doubly excited. Even though Mama hadn't released him from his "down-stay," he jumped up on Razi, who grabbed his front paws and twirled around the room with him.

"All this commotion is making it hard to clear the table," Mama said. "And I need to be early to check the length."

Mama had made the prettiest gossamer skirts for the snowflake dance. Since they had elastic waists, she'd had Keisha try on every one to make sure they had just the right swinginess. But they couldn't touch the floor or else someone might trip.

Keisha picked up the puppy and let him touch the tip of her nose with his tongue. "Shouldn't you be practicing, Razi?"

"I am," Razi said, heel-toeing across the floor. "Listen, Key. It sounds like rain."

"I mean your routine."

Razi stiff-stopped and made his arms rigid. "My *what?*"

"Your routine. What you're gonna do onstage."

"Don't you know anything, Keisha? It's never the same dance twice."

"What's that supposed to mean?"

"It means if you forget . . ." Razi's feet interrupted his mouth with a flurry of tippy-taps. "You just improvise."

"Improvise?"

"You make it up."

"How can you make it up? It's a routine!" Keisha and Rocket had to jump out of the way of Razi's swinging arms.

"Well then . . . look at everybody else and do what they're doing!"

"When I do my routine, it's always the same. Every time. Yours is, too. I've watched you practice."

Razi just rolled his eyes as if Keisha didn't understand anything about performing.

Mama said, "Ada, take Rocket for a quick walk around the block. He'll be in his crate most of the evening."

Keisha pulled on her boots, her coat and her mittens. The late-afternoon sun slanted through the tree branches and glistened on the snow as Rocket attacked every pile that had drifted against a mailbox or bush.

Snatching up a stick, Rocket offered Keisha the other end and began a playful tug-of-war. As they passed the Bakers' fence, Harvey the dog started barking. Since getting a puppy of her own, Keisha had learned that barking was not just barking. It was playful, sad, angry. Harvey was an angry barker, a stay-out-of-my-yard-or-I-might-just-snap-your-nose-off barker. But Keisha suspected he was also a sad barker, an I-never-get-out-of-the-yard-to-go-for-a-walk barker.

Rocket dove behind Keisha, barking back at Harvey. Rocket's name used to be Racket, so Keisha had heard a lot of barking and howling from her coydog. But now that she thought about it, it was hardly ever angry or sad.

"Poor Harvey," Keisha told Rocket. "He has the same routine every day. Wake up, bark at people on the other side of the fence, eat dinner, go to sleep. Wake up. Do it again."

Whoa.

Keisha sat down on a pile of snow, and she didn't even have her snow pants on. She was having a dizzy-making thought. She realized that she'd used the same word—routine—to describe what she did in jump rope, what Razi did in dance class and what Harvey did in the Bakers' yard.

What did that word mean anyway?

Rocket brought her back to her mission by piddling on the Bakers' mailbox. You couldn't clean that up! Keisha piled some snow over the yellow marks and swatted more snow off her bottom. Then she raced Rocket back to the house.

Inside, she wiped Rocket's paws and ran upstairs to change into "going out" clothes. "Can we bring my jump rope?" Keisha asked Mama. Since they only had one vehicle, everybody had to go early with Mama. This guaranteed great seats for the performance, but gave them a lot of time to hang around while Mama made last-minute alterations to the costumes and Ms. Allen and Ms. Perry checked the sound system and gave the children their final instructions.

Mama pulled Keisha's jump rope off the peg by the door and stuffed it in her big purse. "As long as you stay out of the way, I'm sure no one will mind."

Once they'd arrived, Keisha told Grandma she wanted to find a quiet spot to practice her jump rope routine.

That was easier said than done with snowflakes dancing down the halls and stair dancers tapping up and down every step.

"I'm sticking with you," Grandma told Keisha.

"I want to see it for the first time on the big stage."

While Daddy and Paulo practiced walking up the carpeted auditorium steps, Grandma and Keisha found a short hall that no performers seemed to have claimed.

"I'm going to invent a new yoga pose while we're waiting," Grandma said, pressing her palms into the wall. "Are you going to practice your freestyle routine?"

Keisha shook her head. "Not tonight. Right now, I'm going to do the opposite of my routine. I call it . . . 'fun roping,' instead of jump roping."

They could hear the pianist warming up her snowflake music. It sounded like whispers and swinginess. Keisha started to jump to the music, which wasn't like typical routine music with a heavy beat. It was so easy to jump when no one was watching you. Keisha just wanted to feel the music with her jump rope. The snowflakes came out of the piano and whistled past her. She could feel the cold air on her cheeks. It felt like . . . Keisha did an overhand turn and landed in a squat. She

kept jumping from a squat until another swish of wind blew her into a crisscross turn into a scissors kick.

By the time Daddy called to them to take their seats, Grandma had stopped inventing poses and was watching Keisha. But Keisha didn't notice either of them right away. She was a skittering snowflake blowing over a snowy landscape.

The motto at Celia Cruz Performing Arts School was "Jump-stART every day with art!" The mid-winter festival was an old tradition, meant to help everyone remember why they loved snow and ice, since folks in Michigan were getting a little tired of them by mid-February. So the Cruz-ies celebrated with a big concert, featuring the Sensational Snowflake Dancers, the Tremendous Snow-Toe Tappers and the New Orleans Jazzy Winter Wonderland Combo.

The lights went down, and even Paulo stopped his babbling to watch the blue uplights shine through the fog machine. Soon dancers were twirling over the floor in their white leotards and shimmery skirts. Keisha couldn't help it. She swayed in her chair right along with them. Of course, they got a standing ovation. As the stagehands swept up the glitter and snowflakes, Ms. Allen and Ms. Perry rolled out the two staircases. They placed them against one another so the dancers could tap up one side and down the other, just as Keisha had seen the famous dancer Bill "Bojangles" Robinson do in a YouTube video.

The audience took their seats again and grew quiet with anticipation. The first dancer entered stage right. The program said his name was Cyril, and he was about a foot taller than Razi. He moved his feet as if he didn't have shoes on at all. Just slippers. But then Keisha heard the tapping. Razi was right! It sounded like rain. Syncopated rain. The beat from the dancer's shoes traded off with the notes of the piano. Even Cyril's coattails knew how to dance. Swish-tap-slide-tappety-tappety-slide. He hop-hop-hop-tapped up to the top of the stairs and back down again, over and over until he was tapping and stepping and leaping so fast, his feet were a blur. When he finished, he folded his long body into a bow. The audience was silent for a moment—mesmerized—but then they burst into wild applause. You had to stand up and shout and whistle for a performance like that.

The other stair dancers were not as good as Cyril, but each performance had something special. Leah did a split leap; Gordon slid across the floor on his knees; Donald walked up the stairs on his hands.

Razi was the final dancer. It was pretty obvious he

was the young'un. But there was something about the way he sucked on his fingers during a particularly complicated step that made people in the audience nudge one another and point at him. Keisha could tell they thought Razi was beyond adorable.

At the end of his routine, Razi jumped off the steps. Keisha remembered that his big finale was to do a step-tap combination with one foot while he straightened his other leg, making sure it didn't touch the ground. But something happened. Maybe he slipped on a piece of glitter or the bottoms of his shoes were too slide-y; but when he went to do the turn, he just slipped and fell on his behind.

Razi looked around, surprised. He frowned to him-self and sat there, shaking his head "no." Some of his young classmates started to giggle.

It was really about the most embarrassing thing that could happen.

Keisha stood up. Someone had to help Razi!

Grandma put her hand on Keisha's shoulder. "Sit," she whispered. "He knows the show must go on."

Razi looked backstage. "What?" he asked in a stage whisper.

The audience exploded in laughter.

He turned wide-eyed to the audience as if he'd just remembered them. Then he broke into a big perfor-mance smile, rolled onto his back, did a break-dancing turtle-shell spin and hopped to his feet. He finished off by swiggling his hips and doing the disco arms, which Keisha had never seen on any Bill "Bojangles" Robinson YouTube video.

But the audience loved it and Razi got a standing ovation, too.

Later, at Marie Catrib's, Razi was remembering every moment of the evening with a colossally long "and then" story. Since it was his big night, no one inter-rupted him.

"*And then* Ms. Perry said, 'Improvise,' but I thought she said, 'In your *eyes*,' and so I said, 'What?' like *what* is in my eyes, *and then* she said it again." Razi paused, jumped out of his chair and made a stiff bow. "And then I did. The end."

"You were marvelous, Razi," Grandma congratulated him before slurping the last of her raspberry smoothie, complete with one of the travel parasols she kept in her purse in an old cigarette case. "Your future lies in stage and screen."

"I don't know how you think so well on your feet," Big Bob added, pulling off another chunk of carrot cake for Paulo. "I would have frozen."

"But I wasn't on my feet, Big Bob," Razi replied, hopping back into his chair. "Don't you remember? I was on my bottom!"

Chapter 8

"Your mom gave the okay," Daddy told Marcus as he and Keisha stood on the school steps after jump rope practice. "She cleared it with Ms. Tellerico this morning. And Lt. Washington's free, so we can propose your plan to him this afternoon."

"Now? Before we go home?" Keisha wondered why her family could not remember to think of her stomach when making plans after practice.

Daddy tossed a bag of popcorn into the backseat. "This is for the movies."

"I thought you said we were going to the V.A. facility." Marcus caught the bag and tore it open before holding it out to Keisha for the first handful.

"We are. The movies at the V.A. facility. Sarge has something he's dying to show Keisha, and Lt. Washington's not free until five."

As soon as they arrived, Sarge greeted them at the front door and led them to the community room. Keisha could tell he was excited by how fast he was walking.

"Ever since you told me about jump roping, I've gotten interested in the sport," Sarge said as he cued up the video and Keisha, Marcus and Daddy settled into arm-chairs. "I ordered this documentary from the Grand River Library. I've watched it a few times now. It's called *Jump!* and it's about five U.S. teams competing in the world jump rope championships. You're not going to believe what these kids can do."

The screen went black, the music started and what followed was an amazing display of masterful jump rop-ing. When it ended, Keisha and Marcus looked at each other, wide-eyed. Their talking was all over each other: "Did you see what those kids from Houston did in double-Dutch freestyle?" "I didn't know your body could bend like that! He did a flip *over* the top of the rope!" "Even with asthma, she was *first* in single speed. That's dedication."

"Time out, you two!" Daddy said after a bit. "We can't forget our appointment, Marcus. Gather up your drawings and you and I will go see if Lt. Washington is ready to meet with us."

"I'm glad you brought your jump rope," Sarge told Keisha, putting his legs up on the cushions. "Because I have the jump roping bug in a serious way. Will you show me some of the things you do in your routine?"

"After that?" Keisha asked him. "You're sure? It's nothing like what we just saw."

"Now, Keisha. It's good to know what the top of the

mountain looks like. But climbing around base camp is fun, too. Just show me." Sarge waved his arm to dismiss her worries.

Keisha could see he was serious. She pushed the chairs around until she had enough room to show Sarge some of her moves. As she jumped, she explained what she was doing. "You have to show that you can do the basic moves, so everyone puts them into their routine, like this double side-swing and jump, and this. . . ." She kept both legs together as she jumped to the left and to the right. "We call that the skier. The bell is the same thing, but you're jumping forward and back."

Keisha kept jumping, demonstrating straddle, scissors and crossover moves before getting into some slightly harder stuff, like a forward and backward 180, a kick swing and a double peekaboo.

"I'm getting tired just watching you," Sarge laughed.

"You getting her to do your physio for you?" a young woman called out from where she was playing cards with some of the other vets.

"I wish," Sarge called back.

"PFC—that's Private First Class—Simon lost her leg about the same time I did, only she got hers amputated right away," Sarge told Keisha as she moved through her paces. "We've helped each other deal with a lot of things. She's pretty good with her new leg, but she had some brain injuries, too. Now she works with the doctors to improve her short-term memory."

Keisha stopped jumping to catch her breath. "I wonder how you exercise your brain."

Then she remembered something she wanted to tell Sarge. "The other day, when I was listening to them rehearse for Razi's performance, I made up some stuff. Just for fun, like you said. Now that I see how it goes in the big competitions, I realize you can be a lot more creative than we've been."

"Show me what you came up with."

"Well, it was the mid-winter concert and they had these snowflake dancers. It got me thinking. . . ." Keisha stood still for a minute, trying to remember the music. Slowly, she started twirling her rope. Then after a few swings, she started twirling, too, like a snowflake riding the breeze. It started out as a full turn with a heel-to-heel move, but Keisha changed it by using her whole body, dipping and shimmying her shoulders the way the dancers had. Then she transitioned into sort of a combination twist and shuffle, like something she'd seen Razi do. Step-tap-skippety-skippety . . . like a Bojangles snowflake skittering across the ground.

"Whoa!" Marcus was standing in the doorway. "I didn't know you could do a cancan twist and a shuffle at the same time."

Keisha stopped jumping, embarrassed. "How'd it go with Lt. Washington?"

As Marcus gave her a thumbs-up, Sarge said, "Don't stop now. I think you're inventing something new."

"What's that?" Daddy came into the room with Lt. Washington.

"It's nothing, Daddy. Grandma and I were goofing before Razi's performance. I called it fun rope instead of jump rope, and I was showing Sarge how it looked."

"I guess I would call it interpretive jump rope," Sarge said. "You know, like interpretive dance, where you interpret the music with your body. That's what you're doing, Keisha. Only with a jump rope. You should see this, Lieutenant. Hey, don't you play the piano? That's what I heard."

"Well, I used to play some, but I'm out of practice."

"What can you play? Play anything, and maybe Keisha can figure out how it looks in jump rope language."

"Well . . ." Lt. Washington sat down at the piano. "I know some old show tunes." He played a few practice notes. "Can you do something to this?" He began to pound the piano keys and sing: "Oooooooklahoma, where the wind comes sweepin' down the plain."

Keisha looked to Sarge for help.

"Maybe something softer," Sarge suggested. Daddy

and Marcus took a seat and looked at Keisha expectantly. She wished they wouldn't. Suddenly fun roping wasn't so fun.

"Okay, here's something from *The Sound of Music*. Edelweiss, edelweiss . . . um, I don't know any more words. But I can hum it." Lt. Washington pushed up his sleeves.

"Sure. Okay," Sarge told him. "I think she just needs the melody."

Did Sarge understand eye language? Keisha tucked her chin into her collar and looked at him with wide-open eyes.

"Don't think about them, Keisha. Tune in to the music. Tune out everything else."

So Keisha listened to the music. It was high and sweet. After thinking about it, she did a slow side-swing crossover into a grapevine into a twist-360-double-peekaboo. After another twirl, she stepped on her rope.

"That's enough . . . I'm all out of thoughts . . . and I'm dizzy."

"Well, I couldn't see much, but you seemed to get the feel of it," Lt. Washington said as everyone's applause died down. He swung his legs around the piano bench so that he faced them. "We've got some creative kids here, Sarge. You're not going to believe what

Marcus is proposing to keep you occupied—with your furry friend, Larry—for the rest of the winter."

"Who told you about Larry?" Sarge glanced over at Keisha, who shook her head. "I thought that was my secret."

"A good lieutenant understands the needs of his platoon, Sergeant. Recovering is hard work. I'm surprised you haven't named the birds, too, with all the time you have on your hands."

"The cardinal's Gloria," PFC Simon said. "And there's Zenobia, too . . . she's a chickadee."

"The nuthatches are Stalin, Marx and Lenin," added PFC Simon's card-playing partner.

After a good laugh, Daddy said, "The lieutenant has agreed to let us set up a few squirrel-attracting devices. They'll still be in the wild area, in the ravine, but you'll have a good view of them. Our Wild 4-Ever volunteers will keep them stocked with peanuts, so you should be able to see your friends on a regular basis—even when the weather's bad. If all goes well, when the ground thaws, we can install something more permanent."

For a moment, Keisha's thoughts returned to the squirrels at Mt. Mercy. It wasn't just people recovering from injuries who took a liking to wildlife . . . people everywhere did. She and Grandma were pretty certain that Jim the Handyman was using Sister Mary-Lee's peanut stash to make friends with the squirrels. But they didn't want to get him in trouble. Daddy had sealed up all the entry points they could find at Holm-dene Hall, and the Carters were still brainstorming a good solution to the problem of the raining peanuts.

PFC Simon came over to join the conversation. Keisha couldn't believe how well she walked. "Could we help with building it? We hardly ever use the wood shop."

"Excellent thinking on your feet, PFC Simon."

"You mean my *foot*, sir. Or does the fiberglass one count?"

Lt. Washington cleared his throat. "I stand corrected," he said. "Why don't you talk to Private Graham about it? He's a carpenter, isn't he?"

Over the next two weeks, Keisha practiced hard with the jump rope team, and then again with Sarge. While Big Bob, Marcus, Wen, Savannah and any other available Wild 4-Evers built an apparatus for squirrel-feeding fun, she stayed back in the community room, working with Sarge in one corner while some patients watched TV in the other. Since the community room opened onto the new sunroom, people were always walking— or wheeling—in and out to watch the birds flit from feeder to feeder.

Even after a long day of school and practice, she loved to make up new moves and combinations. Sarge seemed to look forward to it, too. Since he'd thought so much about how to get from rock to rock when he had two good legs, he knew really interesting things you could do with your body. And he spent time studying the basic jump rope handbook, so he had lots of ideas when Keisha got there to share the snack that Mama packed for them. Ms. Allen and Ms. Perry sent the recorded music from Razi's concert home with her brother, so that Keisha and Sarge could work on her "fun roping" together. The most interesting part for Keisha was that the moves were not . . . well . . . routine, but different every time. They didn't have to practice it over and over because what they were doing was just for fun.

Keisha "tuned out and tuned in," jumping through the first call for dinner, cheers over the latest basketball victory or arguments over cards. She interpreted the music while Marcus asked PFC Simon about cantilevers—whatever they were—and while Savannah, Marcus and Big Bob demonstrated the springiness of the squirrel bungee jump with a bag of rice from the kitchen. Sometimes, someone even started playing other music on the piano!

It was crazy. But since it was only for fun, it didn't matter.

All this jumping gave Keisha an appetite as big as Daddy's.

"Savannah?" Keisha said one afternoon while they sat waiting for Grandma and Big Bob to say good-bye to the servicemen and women and head home. "When people say they're as hungry as a horse . . . what does that mean? Do horses eat more than other animals?"

"I think it's just because horses are big," Savannah replied. "They don't eat much more than a cow or a pig. At least ours didn't." Whenever she talked about their farm, Savannah got that faraway look that made Keisha think she was picturing Alabama in her mind.

"I like to watch you jump rope," Savannah said, staring out the windows at the birds. At dusk, they were very active. "More the way you do it here than at school. I know this isn't the right way! In dressage, we had to do everything just so or they took off points. But there's something about the way you do your fun roping that reminds me of home."

"I wonder what it is. . . ." Keisha wasn't sure she understood.

Savannah shrugged. "Maybe just bliss."

Keisha looked into Savannah's sad eyes and thought about the apartment her friend had told her about—on the second floor of Savannah's aunt's house.

"Home in Alabama. You know. . . ." Savannah got to her feet and started to snap her fingers. "Sweet home Alabama . . . ," she sang, "where the skies are so blue."

There was something in the way Savannah tried to be cheerful that made Keisha's heart hurt. How hard would it be to leave your dad and half your family and come north with just your mom?

Grandma always said divorce was hard on everybody. It was one thing to know it . . . another to feel it.

"Want to have dinner with us tonight?" Keisha asked Savannah.

"Can I call my mom?"

"Yup. And I can ask my dad. We can work on our Civil War reports. Grandma is the best researcher."

Keisha was one of the few kids she knew who could ask somebody for dinner at the last minute and have their mama be happy about it. Mama was proud of the way she could stretch a meal, and that night, she stretched it to fit Big Bob and Savannah just like that.

They were having harira, Mama's newest soup, and the whole family—even Razi—loved it. Mama had learned to make harira from a Moroccan lady she met at the Mediterranean Island grocery store, which specialized in foods from all over the world. Harira had vegetables and beef, but also other things like garbanzo beans, tomatoes, rice and a big squeeze of lemon. Mama made it just the way the lady told her, only the Carters used the word "chickpeas" instead of "garbanzos" because if you said "garbanzo" in the kitchen, Razi would hop up and down like a kangaroo for just long enough to knock something on the floor.

118

Tonight Mama served the soup with fat breadsticks and showed Savannah how to tear out the soft part and make a spoon you could eat. The warm kitchen, the spicy soup flavored with cinnamon and a spritz of lemon, and lots of conversation and laughter brought some color back to Savannah's cheeks.

"Now . . . back to our squirrel project," Big Bob said, helping himself to another breadstick. "If the weight of an average squirrel is—"

"—between one and two bags of rice." Grandma finished Bob's sentence and slipped a parasol and a pink straw into Savannah's milk. "That's to keep things colorful," she explained.

"I'm just wondering how much spring we need for the diving board when we—"

"You didn't say anything about a swimming pool, Big Bob," Razi blurted out.

"Razi, don't interrupt Big Bob." Daddy took the breadstick plate. "I'm guessing the average squirrel weighs about what this plate weighs. Wait a minute, minus two breadsticks." And to help everyone imagine the average squirrel's weight, he helpfully put the extra-weight breadsticks on his own plate.

"What if the squirrels don't know how to swim? What if they're afraid of the deep end? And then a bigger squirrel named Gregory Thompson pushes them under the water and they can't get—"

"Who is Gregory Thompson?" Mama wanted to know.

"It's a squirrel *playground*, not a pool, Razi. And they'll need some diving-board spring to get up to the dried-corn bungee rope." Grandma twisted the top of her parasol between her fingers, thinking. "What I really want to discuss," she continued, "is Mt. Mercy. I've been doing a little research about squirrels on campus, and I think the folks over at the University of Michigan have come up with a very clever way of handling the 'to feed or not to feed' question."

"Speaking of feeding, are there more breadsticks, Fay? I don't want to take two when the plate hasn't made it around the table for seconds."

Mama smiled at Daddy. "As my father used to say, 'It is the wife who knows her husband.' Check the oven."

"To continue," Grandma said. "Did you know that the club that boasts the most members at the University of Michigan is the squirrel-feeding club?"

"You're kidding, right, Mom?" Daddy had his back to the table since he was pulling the extra breadsticks out of the oven.

"I am *not* kidding. Since we can't re-locate the offending squirrels," Grandma continued after blowing noisily on her soup, "which would be impossible—and cruel at this time of the year, since we'd be forcing them to leave their nests and food stores—this college club's enthusiasm has given me an idea for re-*directing* the Mt. Mercy squirrels away from the administration building *and* helping Ms. Pontell keep the president's rug pristine."

In the rare silence that followed Grandma's pronouncement, Keisha felt a tug on her blouse. "Does your family always talk like this?" Savannah whispered in her ear. "I know you're talkin' English, but I don't have the faintest idea what is going on."

Chapter 9

The USA Jump Rope regional meet was held in Detroit, a city Grandma called the birthplace of civilization since it was the home of the Detroit Tigers, Motown Records and Bommarito's Detroit-style pizza.

In the last year, Keisha had been to Detroit twice. The first time was when the FFGs went to the Detroit Institute of Arts and the Charles H. Wright Museum of African American History. Then last summer, the Carter family spent a whole day going back and forth between the Detroit Science Center and the Children's Museum.

Today's trip was completely different. Keisha and the team would take the bus and stay overnight, while the rest of the Carters would drive separately in the truck and return that evening. Grandma and Big Bob would go in his Bonneville. Though Sarge wanted to come, his doctors weren't sure about extended travel and hours in the bleachers. Grandma had promised to videotape Keisha's routine for him.

The bus got off I-96 and drove through a neighborhood a lot like Alger Heights.

Keisha watched all the buses waiting their turn

to pull in to Central High School. She read the names printed on their sides: Jackson Public Schools, Saginaw Public Schools . . . her tummy did a scissors move with a crisscross turn.

"Okay, Steppers." Coach Rose blocked the aisle as soon as the bus stopped. "Let's remember you are representing Langston Hughes and the city of Grand River today. Be professional, respectful and kind—and don't put your jump ropes down, you'll never find them again! Now . . . let's go win a trophy!" Coach Rose bounced down the bus steps and into the crisp morning air.

Keisha, Aaliyah and Wen joined the mass of jumpers heading into the brick school building. It looked almost like a castle with big, high turrets. Inside,

the Steppers had to line up against the wall by the library while Coach Rose completed team registration. Everyone got a number to pin to their T-shirt. Then they walked two by two into the gym.

Keisha smiled to herself when she saw the huge Central High gymnasium. If Razi were here, he would shout out, trying for an echo. But even echoes would be lost in the sound of hundreds of jumpers stretching out, practicing double Dutch, finding their teammates and getting to know the competition floor. Coach Rose had the Steppers find their home base—the first three bleachers on the visitors' side. That was where they could leave their water bottles, snacks and warm-up jackets when they went to compete.

He handed around the sheet that told when, where and in what event each team member would compete. Keisha was number 2,236. She would perform in double-Dutch speed first and single speed in the early afternoon, and she was the last slot in the final freestyle event.

What a drag! Her tummy would be crisscrossing all day long as she saw and heard about the other jumpers.

"Let's do a lap and see everything." Wen grabbed Keisha's hand and tugged her along.

"Wait for us!" Keisha turned to see Marcus, Jorge and Aaliyah hopping up and down, trying to find them in the crowd.

Marcus still had a pencil stuck behind his ear from when he was doodling on the bus. "Hey, do you think at lunchtime Coach will let me go outside and draw this building? It looks like a European castle!"

The Steppers managed to make it all the way around the gym by forming a line and grabbing the shoulder of the person in front of them. When they got back to home base, it was time for them to split up and go to their separate events.

Keisha, Aaliyah and Wen started off strong in double-Dutch speed. As it turned out, Aaliyah's booming voice was a big plus in a room with all that noise. She and Wen twirled furiously for Keisha, helping her get a personal best. With Aaliyah's and Wen's quick skipping, their threesome advanced to the finals.

Marcus and Jorge also advanced in boys' single speed jumping. Though Keisha didn't make it, Wen—who'd been working hard on her wrist motion—moved up to the final heat along with Aaliyah, who also made it to the finals in double unders.

They had never seen such tough competition. During warm-up, Keisha watched the jumpers from Flint's Eisenhower Elementary Cadettes and Detroit's Campbell Elementary Buzzing Bees. Their skipping was fierce. The Detroit jumpers used old-school style, sitting back low during the speed events and pumping with their knees. It was faster, but it made your thighs just burn!

Though she tried not to make a big deal of it, Keisha's freestyle routine stayed in the back of her mind like a thistle bur all day long. At three in the afternoon, she was stretching and doing some warm-up skipping when Coach managed to pull together everyone who wasn't involved in a heat.

"You have done your school and your city proud today," he said. "Three personal bests! We can go back to Langston Hughes with our heads held high."

"But it's not over yet!" Marcus said. "Maybe we'll bring home a trophy."

"That's what I wanted to talk to you about," Coach said. He pushed his baseball cap back on his head. "According to my calculations"—he glanced at his clipboard—"you would have to have three firsts in the final round to land in the top three. Looking at the splits here, Marcus and Aaliyah have a chance in speed jumping . . . and *maybe* Aaliyah can edge out those crazy jumpers from Saginaw in the double unders. . . ." Coach stopped talking and stared at the wall, lost in thought.

How did Keisha know he was comparing her routine—the one she would perform in less than half an hour—with the difficulty of the other routines to see how much of a chance she had to place?

Did she know it because that's what *she* was thinking?

Maybe everyone was thinking the same thing.

Keisha had been the best freestyler on the team, but her play-it-safe routine would not gain them enough points, even if she nailed every hop, skip and jump.

"We have to leave room for possibility," Coach said. "We have no idea how well the other freestylers will perform, and Keisha hasn't jumped yet."

When Coach dismissed them, Keisha tried to do some belly breathing, but her breath got all stopped-up in her middle somewhere. She knew even if she nailed her routine, her moves wouldn't put her in the top tier. The others would have to mess up big-time! It wouldn't happen. Keisha didn't even wish for that.

She bit her lip. If she hadn't been so nervous all the time, she could have practiced a harder routine! This routine was an elbow bone, not a backbone.

Someone came up behind her and covered her eyes. "Don't turn around too fast," the person whispered. "Or you'll tip me over."

Keisha turned around slowly and gave a squeal. "How did you get in here?" she asked, giving Sarge a big hug. "And what about your leg?"

"It's fake! Didn't I tell you? No, it was fine. I used a lot of pillows. And to get in, your coach gave me this." Sarge held up a registration badge. "I have a confession to make, Keisha. Your dad gave me Coach Rose's phone number, and I called him up a while ago to tell him about the fun roping you've been doing. And guess what? I brought the music from Razi's show."

Keisha looked up at Sarge, confused. She sat down on the bleachers. Sarge sat next to her.

Coach Rose came and sat down beside them. Keisha could see the rest of the Steppers hanging around in the

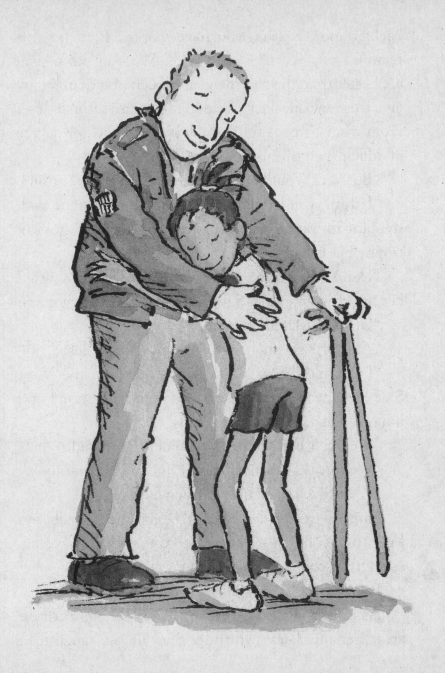

background. "Keisha, you have worked hard for this team for two years," Coach said. "We both know you are better than the routine you've been practicing. I say give this new one a try. We don't have anything to lose. From what Sarge is telling me, there's a greater degree of difficulty in this routine."

"But . . ." Would fun roping be fun in competition?

"I think you should do it, too, Key," Marcus said, stepping forward. "And not just so we can bring home a trophy but because it's fun to watch."

"Here's why *I* think you should do it." Aaliyah jutted out her chin and walked toward them like an Egyptian.

"Uh-oh." Marcus poked Jorge.

"Aaliyah's gettin' her swagger on," Jorge teased.

"I say, let's show 'em how it's done on the West Side." Aaliyah leaned back, pumping her arms and hula-hooping.

"We don't live on the West Side," Jorge said.

"We sure do." Aaliyah gave Jorge her all-that look.

"West Side of Michigan," Wen explained.

Sarge tugged on the lapels of his jacket. "Coach says I get to put the music in, and that means I'll have my usual front-row seat at one of your performances."

Performance.

As Keisha walked over to the freestyle-competition area, her mind was whirling. She almost ran into a

Buzzing Bee. Competing made her mess up, but performing was all about the flow. And if she was going to try to get a higher score, she had to do something . . . more.

Keisha tapped the tape on the competition square three times for good luck. Then she took her place. "Judges ready?" she asked.

They nodded. No one was even looking at her. They were all finding the right form, checking the number on her shirt and filling in her name and school. Keisha nodded to Sarge, who was standing by the CD player.

The music from Razi's mid-winter recital was so different from the pounding beat of other jumpers' music that afterward, Keisha told Sarge that might have been what helped her most. How could you call this competing?

Keisha stood completely still, listening to the music and waiting for the first cold breeze. It whirled around her, and then, after a few jumps, she became airborne herself: scudding, rolling, swaying, soaring. Just the way a snowflake would feel on a crisp, sunny winter afternoon, floating near the river, passing the squirrels and the joggers and the children on the swing set in their shiny plastic boots. Keisha translated—from cold to skip, from blow to kick, from flutter to swing. Then, almost as soon as she'd begun, she was finished. She drifted down onto the top hat of a snowman and took a bow, blinking at the crowd.

People leapt to their feet in the bleachers. Keisha could see Grandma shouting into a megaphone, but she couldn't hear her over the roar of the crowd.

Coach Rose grabbed her up in a big bear hug and walked her over to Sarge. As they passed the judges' table, Keisha heard snatches of their conversation: "—take us to an exciting new level . . ." "—never thought about doing it without a downbeat . . ." "How am I supposed to score this? I don't even know what she was doing. Can you name every one of those tricks?"

Sarge was the next person to give her a hug. "I've never seen you look so graceful," he said. But Keisha barely had time to respond before she was swept away by her teammates.

"You were definitely in the flow," Marcus told her.

"That was sweet!" Jorge clapped Keisha on the back.

"Say, 2,236!" It was the captain of the Buzzing Bees. "What was that move you did when you—" She stopped, swung her rope in a circle and did a backward somersault, but she got caught up in the rope.

"Um . . ." Keisha giggled. "Larry-recovers-from-missing-the-branch."

If Grandma could name her yoga poses, why couldn't Keisha name her new moves?

"What about this one?" The Cadettes' captain tried to shuffle her feet and skip her rope between each short step.

"That's . . . that's my calabaza steptaraza."

"Your what?"

"That's how we lay it down on the West Side," Aaliyah said, pointing at the floor.

"It's Grand River–style stepping," Wen chimed in.

Keisha's energy didn't flow quite as easily in the final round, since there was more pressure on her to perform. More people watching made Keisha more aware of what she was doing. To calm herself, she pictured her friends at the V.A. facility. These people were just like them . . . curious to see her routine. Besides, they wouldn't know if she messed up or not because even *she* didn't know exactly what she was going to do ahead of time.

It was almost dark before the final round was over. The Steppers would wait until all the scores were tallied and announced, then stay overnight at the Renaissance Center. At their hotel, skippers from all over the state could go to special rooms and meet each other and share moves. But Mama and Daddy were anxious to get on the road.

Just before they left, Daddy grabbed Keisha's hand and led her over to the cove by the drinking fountains. Coach Rose followed them. "Honey, Coach wants to talk to us about something. It seems a few of the coaches are contesting your scores."

Coach Rose got down on one knee to be closer to Keisha. "When someone contests a score that would make a difference in a team's placement, the videotapes have to be reviewed by an independent panel of judges. That won't happen this afternoon. It could take a few weeks for a final decision."

Keisha looked back and forth between her dad and her coach. "So we won't know today?"

"I don't think so." Coach Rose patted Keisha on the back. "For now, let's be proud of our achievements. Whether they allow your routine or not, Keisha, you definitely learned that you can jump with the best of them."

Daddy kissed the top of Keisha's head. "There's no doubt in my mind that *my* girl helped put the Grand River Steppers in the center of the radar screen for Michigan jumpers."

That evening, the whole team gathered in the

Coach Insignia restaurant on the seventy-second floor of the RenCen. The Steppers rushed to the windows and oohed and aahed at the lights of Windsor, Ontario, across the Detroit River.

Standing there, Keisha felt a shiver of pleasure run down her spine. At dinner, everyone had wanted to talk to her. She was a jumping sensation! Even if they disqualified her for not sticking to the same routine, jumpers from all over the state wanted to learn more about her moves. Fun roping was launched.

"Want a Lemonhead?" Aaliyah pressed up next to her friend and held out a box.

"Where did you get those?"

"They have a vending machine filled with candy on every floor." Wen handed Keisha two Pixy Stix while Aaliyah filled her other palm with Lemonheads.

Keisha put six Lemonheads in her mouth at once. She stood shoulder-to-shoulder with her best friends and let her eyes leave the colored lights of the city and float up to the blanket of twinkling stars above. It was one of those sweet-and-sour moments she'd never forget.

Chapter 10

One week later, a few Wild 4-Evers gathered at the V.A. facility to celebrate the opening of the Wild 4-Ever Squirrel Circus, starring—hopefully—Larry and all his friends. They kneeled in front of the window—Aaliyah, Jorge, Marcus, Razi, Savannah, Wen, Zack and Zeke—so that they didn't block anyone's view. Keisha was next to Sarge on the couch. PFC Simon brought her binoculars so she could see everything and describe it for the vets who couldn't see as well.

Everyone watched anxiously as Lt. Washington made his way down the ravine. As director, he had insisted on putting in the first load of peanuts. Keisha looked over the contraption they'd erected a few days earlier. There were long, thin pieces tied between trees for the high-wire act; a bicycle wheel hooked on to the end of a bouncy cord for the bungee jump; and a homemade paddle wheel with wooden cups that they hoped would act like a Ferris wheel. The squirrels would be doing the same things they did in the trees, but now they would be doing them in full view of the veterans. And because the Squirrel Circus was in the ravine, separate from the bird-feeding station, the squirrels would get their corn and peanuts and leave the seeds for the birds.

"Can squirrels smell?" Razi asked. "Do they know the peanuts are coming?"

"I don't think they can smell them inside the bag," Big Bob said. "We should probably get out the checkerboard and give them some time to sniff out the food."

"Lt. Washington just slipped," PFC Simon reported. "Now he's sliding down the ravine on his butt."

The vets who could stand gave Lt. Washington a standing ovation.

"It means a lot to the troops that Lt. Washington is doing this," Sarge told Keisha. "But I think we might have to figure out an easier way to place the peanuts. We don't want *him* recovering from injuries, too."

"I'm on it." Marcus whipped out his drawing pad and started sketching the area.

"I hope there aren't any squirrels over two pounds," Wen fussed. "That was our weight-test limit. I wouldn't want *them* to get injured, either."

"Squirrels definitely don't test every branch they jump onto for safety first." PFC Simon continued to peer through her binoculars.

"I've got a good feeling about this." Sarge had pushed himself up and made his way slowly toward the window. Keisha followed him. "I think Larry's going to show up."

The group fell silent as they watched Lt. Washington open the big bag of peanuts and load the pail. He hoisted it high in the air. Then he took another bag, filled with dried corncobs, and clamped six cobs on to the spokes of the bike wheel before pulling on the rope and raising it twenty feet off the ground.

"I get to be red, Big Bob." Razi had forgotten all about the squirrels and was taking fistfuls of checkers out of a box from the game cupboard.

"Let's wait a few for the games," Daddy said. "You never know. Lt. Washington spilled some peanuts as he loaded them, and he's climbing back up the hill now."

"I'll play with you, Razi." Zeke jumped up from his place by the window.

"Okay. It's my turn."

"Don't we have to set up the game board first?"

"Wait a minute. I think I see one." PFC Simon was so excited, she hopped up and down on her good foot and started to wobble.

"Careful!" Sarge almost tipped over trying to make sure PFC Simon didn't hurt herself.

Wen came up behind Keisha and nudged her in a do-you-see-what-I-see way as Sarge took his time releasing PFC Simon's shoulder.

"Oh darn! It's just a paper lunch bag blowing up the hill."

Lt. Washington came into the sunroom, still brushing burs off his coat. "We will definitely be figuring out a better access point," he said, squinting into the late-afternoon sun. "PFC Simon, have you identified the target?"

"One lunch bag, sir, and not a squi— Hey, wait a minute . . . is that Larry? Awaiting positive identification. Sarge?"

Sarge pressed his forehead against the big glass window. "I can't say if it's Larry. I *can* identify it as a member in good standing of the Grand River squirrel community."

The Wild 4-Evers, who'd been at ease eating Grandma's homemade caramel corn, snapped to attention.

Suddenly he was on the platform. "Oh, he's a big one," Wen said. "I hope he doesn't weigh more than—"

"Two pounds!" Zack and Zeke said together.

"There's not much we can do now," Zack said, pointing. "He's getting ready to launch."

"Cross your fingers just in case," Zeke added. Both boys crossed their fingers behind their backs.

The squirrel sat up on his haunches. Was he sniffing the air?

"Ready, set . . . ," Marcus encouraged him. As if he knew he had an audience, the furry little guy bounded along the thin strip of wood and pounced on the pail. His back legs dangled in the air for a moment.

"Liftoff!" Razi called out. "To the moon!"

Later, as he was recounting it for Mama, who'd stayed home so Paulo could finish his nap, Razi described the first-ever Squirrel Circus performance in great "and then" detail. "*And then* he hung from the pail *and then* he dropped down onto the corncob wheel *and then* the other one bounced on the peanut butter pinecone bungee cord *and then* . . ."

Keisha didn't mind listening to Razi's play-by-play because Rocket was asleep on her lap and she was giving his velvety ears a good massage.

"They're earning their treats, believe me," Daddy said. "It was worth it to see the vets' faces. Everyone was having a good time! Sarge pointed out to Lt. Washington what good role models squirrels were, trying over and over to achieve their goals. He suggested a video feed to the physio room, for when he needed encouragement to keep going with his hamstring curls."

Paulo watched everyone's enthusiasm with wide eyes, his thumb firmly stuck in his mouth. He was still waking up.

"I think I'll take Paulo with me tomorrow instead of going to Story Time," Mama said. "I'd like to see this for myself."

"Well, Mr. Adorable might be competition for Larry and the gang." Daddy reached over and ruffled Paulo's hair.

Grandma bustled into the kitchen, pulling on her jacket. "Do Keisha and I have time before dinner to run out to Mt. Mercy and see how our squirrel-diversion plan is going?"

Mama checked the oven timer and nodded. She put some molasses cookies in a plastic bag to keep Keisha's stomach company on the drive to the campus.

* * *

"I wanted a little private time with you," Grandma told
Keisha as they drove. "We need to have a Grandma-
Granddaughter Talk."

"With a capital T?" Keisha asked. When Grandma
and Keisha had a capital T Talk, it was usually something interesting—like finding your bliss or how to
make a six-minute chocolate cake so you could celebrate at the drop of a hat—what Grandma called the big
kahunas in life. But any other kind of talk was usually
more along the lines of a Grandma Professor lecture.

"Capital, italicized, double-underlined T," Grandma
said as she pulled into the main entrance at Mt. Mercy.

"Got it." Keisha had never had one of those.

Grandma didn't stop at the administration building
this time. Instead, she drove around it, past the dormito-
ries and into a sheltered woodsy area by the field house.

She turned off the truck and shifted to face Keisha.
"You are growing into an amazing young lady: doing
your schoolwork, working on your jumping, babysitting
Paulo and helping with the family business. . . . I'm so
proud of you."

Grandma opened the truck door and stepped onto
the snowy road. Keisha followed her along a paved trail
that led into the woods.

"I was beginning to wonder if you were having enough fun." Grandma reached into her inside jacket pocket and pulled out a bag of peanuts still in their shells. "But when I watched you practice your fun roping, I felt like you understood, on a very deep level, how work and fun can blend together to make . . . hmmmm . . . how can I say this? A delicious life. I hope you keep what you've learned through this experience close to your heart." Grandma tore open the bag and counted out six peanuts. She handed them to Keisha.

"I'm not just talking about your nerves. I'm talking about dreaming up creative solutions to difficult problems. It was you who suggested Jim the Handyman was feeding the squirrels after noticing how happy he was when he talked about them. *You* who invented the Squirrel Circus. Others helped, yes, but you did the lion's share of the work. And *you* who came up with the snowflake routine.

"Things don't always work out the way we want them to—we have no idea what the judges will decide. But what happened to you in this process is so much bigger than lugging home a trophy."

Keisha stared at the peanuts in her hand, letting all of Grandma's words sink in. About Jim, she thought it might get lonely working by yourself all day in boiler rooms and up on roofs. And if it hadn't been for her, all those crazy pieces of wood would have ended up in a bonfire. As for the fun roping, Sarge had helped a lot.

Keisha leaned into her grandma. The sun was setting, and even though Grandma's words made her feel warm inside, her outside was getting cold. "Where are we going? Is it much farther?"

"We're almost there, sweetie. In fact . . ." Grandma looked around as if she was expecting someone. "We are here."

"Where?"

"In the Mt. Mercy Natural Area."

"So this is where people feed the squirrels now?"

Grandma nodded. "It's not by any buildings, so if you're afraid of squirrels—or allergic to peanuts—you never need to come here."

"Has it helped keep the squirrels away from the administration building?"

"That's what Mr. Fox called to tell us today. The newly formed Mt. Mercy Squirrel-Feeding Club started close to the administration building and, each day, fed the squirrels a little farther away until they got here. Mr. Fox said there will be only so many peanuts given out for feeding each day. That's why I only gave you six."

Keisha popped a peanut out of its shell. "Otherwise, they'd get a squirrel population explosion."

"Right. But students and staff were bound to feed

the squirrels anyway. This way, with a club, they'll be able to discourage it on other parts of the campus and at other times. . . . You'll see what I mean in a minute. I want you to experience this by yourself, so turn around. I'm going to count to fifty and then call you. Start walking toward me and wave your peanuts."

Grandma counted very loudly. When she reached fifty, Keisha turned around. It was easy to see Grandma's puffy pink coat and color-coordinated hat and mittens about a quarter mile away. Keisha hopped from one foot to the other to warm up. She started to walk slowly toward Grandma, holding out her peanuts.

She hadn't taken five steps before a squirrel rushed out to the side of the path and sat up on his haunches. He tilted his head as if to say: *Have you got something for me?*

Keisha did as Grandma had instructed and held on to her peanuts. A few feet down the path, another squirrel joined the first one. Then another and another until it was a lineup of squirrels, sitting on their hind feet. Some waved their paws as if they wanted Keisha to throw the peanuts to them. Others chattered and flicked their bushy tails, but there was no doubt about it—Keisha and her peanuts were the main attraction.

Grandma walked back and met her halfway. "It's a squirrel parade," she said, holding out her arms in a "ta-da!" "They're giving you a standing ovation. Now take a bow for winning the title of this year's Grand River Snowflake Jump Rope Queen from Langston Hughes Elementary."

Keisha giggled. It was just like Grandma to create a squirrel parade in her honor. She held up a peanut. "Can I feed them now?"

"I promised we'd only use a dozen. I'll take mine further down the way."

As soon as Grandma disappeared around the bend, Keisha tossed one peanut. She felt like Mr. Drockmore as she looked around at all the fat, healthy squirrels

waving their paws as if to say, *Choose me! Choose me!*

Mt. Mercy was a good place to live if you were a squirrel. So was the V.A. facility. In fact, so was just about anywhere in Grand River, Michigan.

Keisha chose another squirrel and tossed out a second peanut. There was a scramble for the nut before all the attention turned back to her. She kind of liked being the center of attention now. For the benefit of her audience, Keisha did a short impromptu performance. She skipped, she hopped, she crisscross-kicked the snow. And for her final trick, she did a scissors leap and tossed all the peanuts in the air. Then she bowed to her furry audience and said, "The end."

Squirrel Fact File

• Squirrels are rodents that live from three to five years in the wild, on average. There are ten species of tree squirrels in the United States. They range in size from the small red squirrel (about 12 inches from head to tail and weighing around half a pound) to the big fox squirrel (it grows up to 28 inches long and reaches 2.5 pounds). The gray squirrel is the most common American squirrel.

• Squirrels eat a variety of things, most often nuts (especially acorns), seeds, bark, twigs, roots and bulbs. They bury nuts and seeds under soil to save for when food is scarce. No one is quite sure how squirrels find these "caches." Some researchers believe squirrels use their memory, relying on landmarks. The most popular theory is that squirrels use their excellent sniffers—even when the food is under many feet of snow!— to locate their hidden stashes.

• Squirrels need to protect themselves from the cold, so they look for cavities—like in old trees—to nest in during the winter months. Your attic is a good-looking cavity to a squirrel. Trim tree branches away from the house; keep holes patched with metal (squirrels can chew through wood and plastic); and don't leave food outdoors, since it will attract squirrels.

• Squirrels' long, bushy tails come in handy in a number of ways. First,

WHATEVER THE DILEMMA, IF IT'S GOT FUR OR FEATHERS (OR SCALES!),
THE CARTERS ARE THE ONES TO CALL!

the tails help them balance as they scamper along tree branches. Squirrels also use their tails to keep them warm and to shade them in sun. In addition to chattering, squirrels communicate by shaking their tails, too.

• Hawks, owls and snakes prey on squirrels, but their biggest "predator" may be the automobile.

• Though lots of people enjoy feeding squirrels, it's not a great idea to get too close. Squirrels have good vision, but their eyes are on the sides of their heads. They can't see what's at the tip of their nose, so they might nibble your finger instead of the peanut!

Dear Readers,

You may not believe me when I tell you this, but I got the idea for a squirrel interrupting job interviews because it happened to me! I wasn't sure what to do. No one addresses this in any of the "how to ace your interview" articles. I finally pointed it out, and the interviewer said just what Mr. Fox says in the book—"I don't want to hurt it. I just want it to go away!"

Squirrels can be a real challenge. A former tenant in our old farmhouse used to open seventy-five-pound bags of sunflower seeds and dump them in the driveway for the squirrels. When we moved in more than ten years ago, those squirrels were not happy that we didn't open bags for them, too. In fact, they came up and scolded me through the screen door. After a while, they forgot about the food and settled for chewing holes in our house and nesting in our attic. We live-trapped three little red squirrels while I was writing this book! As soon as we find the holes and patch them, they chew new ones.

We've also got great squirrels at the newly renovated park area next to our Grand Rapids Home for Veterans and in Riverside Park. When I'm rollerblading along the river,

I sometimes pretend they are lining up to watch me—they're really hoping I'm one of those people who throw peanuts—and I bow to them just like Keisha does.

As we writers like to say to one another, "Show, don't tell." In *Show Time* I've tried to show you all the ways I've seen squirrels make mischief. I bet you could show me a few more.

Happy reading!
Sue

P.S. There really is a squirrel-feeding club at the University of Michigan. Visit it online at www.michigansquirrels.com.

P.P.S. To keep seed stealers from our bird feeders, we've mounted squirrel baffles on the feeder poles. These metal cones are easy to install and keep squirrels from climbing up the poles. But very determined squirrels can sometimes get around them. Raccoon baffles are a longer version. That's what finally worked with the crazy squirrels on our property.

Acknowledgments

I would like to thank my family—my sons, Max and Walter Gilles, and my husband, Roger (who have trapped and relocated more than their fair share of critters). Also the national organization USA Jump Rope for bringing this cool sport to more schools. Visit it online at www.usajumprope.org. Click on "Watch Our All-Star Demo" to see jump rope performances that defy gravity.

About the Author

Sue Stauffacher lives with her husband and sons in a 150-plus-year-old farmhouse in the city of Grand Rapids, Michigan. Over the years, possums, bats, raccoons, mice, squirrels, crows, ducks, woodchucks, chipmunks, voles, skunks, bunnies, and a whole bunch of other critters have lived on the property. Though Sue is not a rehabilitator herself, she is passionate about helping kids know what to do when the wild meets the child.

Sue's novels for young readers include *Harry Sue, Donutheart,* and *Donuthead,* which *Kirkus Reviews* called "touching, funny, and gloriously human" in a starred review. Her most recent picture book, *Nothing but Trouble,* won the NAACP Image Award for Outstanding Literary Work—Children. Besides writing children's books, Sue is a frequent visitor to schools as a speaker and literacy consultant, drawing on two decades of experience as a journalist, educator, and program administrator. To learn more about Sue and her books, visit her on the Web at www.suestauffacher.com.